Clamp

Peter K.K. Williams

ISBN-13 978-1-60145-281-8
ISBN-10 1-60145-281-0

Printed in the United States of America.

Library of Congress # TXu1-342-321

The Kieron Press
Burlington, Vermont
Kieronpress.com
2007

Clamp

Peter K.K. Williams

Chapter One

The windowless concrete cube dematerialized as fog wafted in from the bay, silently enveloping the pumping facility in an opaque gray shroud. Cold drizzle swirled around the solitary figure climbing the metal stairs attached to the structure's south wall. There, twenty feet above the ground, unrelieved by the slightest gesture of architectural frivolity, a steel door painted green was the only way in or out. The man selected a key from a ring attached to his belt, unlocked the door and pushed. Rusty hinges grated, the screech instantly swallowed by the gloom of a miserable dying day.

Thad Steady stepped into the concrete carapace and pulled the door shut behind him with a resounding clang. Only a hissing sound from within the structure defied the silence. His flashlight beam lanced the control room with quick nervous stabs. Beads of condensation glistened on the cement walls, reflecting pinpoints of light like the eyes of countless watchful spiders.

The hydrologist sniffed the dank, chlorine-tainted air. Then he removed a small metal cylinder from a jacket pocket, opened the regulator's valve and watched as the rubber hose tensed under pressure. He placed the mouthpiece between his lips and inhaled, shuddering as stale compressed air filled his lungs. The breather held a ten-minute supply, more than enough to allow him to determine what had triggered the alarm that had summoned him from his Lazy Boy recliner and the final quarter of the football game on television.

Thad Steady approached a rectangular panel studded with status indicator lights – all shining bright green except for one glass bezel that glared as red as a Cyclopean eye.

Looks like we got trouble in the pulse generator, he decided, reaching out to hit a switch on the wall. The naked 100-watt bulb suspended overhead flared brightly, emitted a faint popping sound and died, plunging the control room back into darkness.

Somewhere deep in the bowels of the plant a timer triggered the release of a retaining pin. Gravity immediately accelerated a heavy steel piston down the length of an inclined track. The piston then struck a metal plate welded to a stainless steel holding tank… BOOM! Like the hammering of some forgotten evil, a balrog perhaps, trapped in Tolkien's fabled mines of Moria, the noise resonated ominously before subsiding.

Sounds like the acoustic pulse is working just fine, he thought, but that red warning light on the panel says otherwise.

Thad Steady knew every inch of the system, having designed and supervised its construction. He alone understood its needs and the subtleties of its caprices. Good job security, he knew, but somewhat of a burden having to be permanently on call – day and night – obliged to drop everything at a moment's notice to attend to the slightest malfunction, whether on his wife's birthday or on a bitter subzero January morning.

The acoustic pulse was a normal part of the plant's daily operation, the sound occurring once every three minutes when the system entered a new purge cycle. Each time the heavy piston slammed against the impact plate the resulting shock wave spread through the cistern and killed whatever tiny intruders had managed to slither into the sluice. Once slain, the tiny roundworms and nematodes were much easier to flush away. After all, no one wanted creepy-crawlies wriggling in their drinking water.

After each pulse, a retractor motor hauled the hammer back up the ramp to await the next release.

"Mighty peculiar," muttered Thad Steady as he inspected the circuit breakers. None had tripped, even though the red eye on the panel continued its unblinking stare. He pointed the flashlight at the floor ahead and walked to a descending flight of stairs, following the beam's bright spot as he moved deeper into the plant's viscera. His work boots clattered dully on each metal step. The hydrologist paused to check a thermometer attached to the wall. The air temperature within the structure remained equal to the water temperature at the surface of the lake. A sober 52 degrees. Not bad on dry land, but fraught with hypothermic peril for anyone careless enough to fall into the water.

A twinge of claustrophobia pricked the back of Thad Steady's mind when he reached the system's lowest level, an unlit corridor that narrowed as he walked beneath ganglia of pipes and ducts. He approached the purge reservoir – the killing chamber where countless insignificant lives were snuffed out every day – a cistern that rose chest high. As he watched, the retaining pin snapped back, the metal piston hurtled down the rail and slammed against the impact plate... BOOM!

"Take that, you slimy little bastards," Thad exulted as the sound reverberated. The retractor motor whined as it hauled the heavy piston back up the incline. When the pin re-engaged, the pulse-hammer was once again armed.

A glance at the luminous dial of his watch, but in that split-second of inattention, the flashlight slid from his grasp, hit the floor and blinked out.

Suddenly engulfed by impenetrable blackness, another probing tendril of claustrophobia awakened a long-forgotten episode from Thad's childhood. In 1957, when little Thaddeus was eight years old, he and his young friends had come upon a newly installed drainage conduit built alongside their favorite stretch of brook; a place where development was about to transform the land from rural to suburban. Shaped like a small butte, the concrete mound jutted a yard above the dirt. The boys gathered around its open maw, a circular aperture not yet covered by a steel plate, and then peered down at the steel rungs that descended into darkness.

"Okay, who's goin' in first?" asked Buzzy, the group's leader and an incipient bully. "What about you, Thad, or are ya' chicken?"

"I'll show you who's chicken," Thaddeus replied as he stepped forward and lowered a Keds-shod foot onto the top rung. The other kids watched silently as he descended into a dark abyss made all the more intense by the contrast between brilliant sunshine and the lightless void beneath. They followed, one by one, but only Thaddeus was equipped that day with an official Cub Scout penlight.

He reached the bottom and began to crawl on hands and knees through the horizontal conduit that stretched into black infinity. Another access shaft waited 300 feet away, although it seemed more like miles. The intrepid spelunkers inched forward – each convinced he was about to drown like a rat in a sudden surging flood.

Thaddeus had crawled less than 30 feet when the 1.5-volt battery in his penlight began to die. The light slowly faded to a feeble yellow... then vanished.

The boy froze, pupils dilated to the max, trapped within a reverberant concrete cylinder into which no photon of daylight would ever intrude. Claustrophobia suddenly lurched out of the darkness like a hungry Komodo dragon and seized him in its septic jaws, evoking a shrill scream. Nothing is as contagious as panic and mindless, primal fear overwhelmed the group. Unable to turn around, the boys fought – yelling and kicking and clawing at the abrasive walls of their tomb until their fingers, knuckles and knees were scraped raw and bloody.

The struggle lasted only a minute, although it felt like an eternity. They inched their way back the way they'd come, ever closer to the dim penumbra of light that marked the entrance to the vertical shaft and their salvation, emerging bruised and dazed into the radiant sunshine resonant with the drone of locusts.

The memory faded as Thad Steady groped at his feet for the flashlight. He grabbed it and disassembled it as efficiently as a blindfolded Marine breaking down a carbine. He installed the spare bulb stored in the device's end-cap. A push of the button and a powerful beam of light punctured the darkness.

"That's better," he muttered, wiping the sheen of cold sweat from his brow with a sleeve. He checked his watch. Enough air remained in the breather for another five minutes. The next acoustic pulse was due at any moment and so he waited. But nothing happened.

A quick glance at a gauge told him the purge reservoir was full, and that alone should've set off the next cycle. The pressure sensor must be clogged, he decided. To test his theory, he placed his right foot on top of the striker plate, boosted himself up and pointed the light at the water. That's odd, he thought, leaning out to get a closer look; instead of a smooth untroubled surface, the water churned with turbulence.

Suddenly his foot slipped off the impact-plate and he fell, slamming his shin against the metal protuberance. "Goddamn it to hell!" he shouted.

Without warning the locking pins snapped back, the piston plunged down and struck his left kneecap, shattering it as effectively as a hammered walnut. Once again, he dropped the flashlight, but this time it splashed into the water and sank to the bottom where it came to rest pointing upwards. Thad Steady gasped at the pain that dwarfed the contusion on his right shin to insignificance. He used his right leg to lurch clear of the murderous impact mechanism but misjudged his position and whacked his forehead firmly against the concrete ceiling, knocking himself out cold.

The man slumped into the cistern's 52-degree water. The respirator slid out from between his lips as the weight of absorbent clothing dragged him under. Only his plaid hunting cap remained afloat as his lungs filled with water. His brain began to expire at a rate considerably faster than the batteries in his waterproof flashlight. But before they, too, died and joined Thaddeus Steady in the great hereafter, the flashlight beam projected writhing shadows onto the chamber's cement ceiling.

Chapter Two

The little town of Krampton sat on a stretch of the eastern shore of Lake Champlain, midway along its 110-mile length at a point where the lake attains its maximum width of five miles. Incorporated in 1763, Krampton was founded by a hardy passel of German immigrants, trappers and farmers – all intent upon carving a niche in the howling colonial wilderness. The town supported several dairy farms, a lumber mill, a bar, an exclusive luxury resort, a general store and a rock 'n roll band known as Squirrels in the Attic.

The population included residents who endured all twelve months of the year and the snowbirds that migrated up for the brief summer season. Between them, the people were kept busy growing crops, growing children or simply growing old.

As in many of the 250 hamlets and villages that dot the Vermont map like so many flyspecks, Krampton's graveyard nestled alongside the church, the church spire loomed above the town hall and the town hall stood adjacent to the general store: A veritable holy trinity – the sacred, the profane and the convenient – death, taxes, groceries – all in one handy location.

The church notwithstanding, the Krampton Kountry formed the nucleus around which daily life revolved, the central node where news and gossip were exchanged. The store sat between two ancient towering elms, vast shady umbrellas that continued to miraculously evade the scourge of Dutch elm disease. Twenty miles to the east, beyond fields devoted alternatively to corn and alfalfa, a wisp of cloud snagged the tip of General Stark Mountain – one of many vertebrae in the curved spine of the Green Mountains.

A mile inland from the lake, a lone figure walked along a dirt road. Tom Snee pushed an old balloon-tire bicycle, always on foot, never actually riding. He was only 57 but looked every minute of 75. Gaunt and grizzled, he wore a battered straw hat to shade his dome. Although the day was warm, he wore a greasy parka over a tie-dyed T-shirt and a pair of baggy trousers held up by a bit of rope tied around the waist. Worn out sneakers protected his feet and a pair of cheap wrap-around sunglasses hid eyes as blue as cat's eye marbles.

Snee was an artist. Everyone in Krampton had seen him trudging along, scrounging for empty beer cans or an interesting or useful item – a shiny chestnut perhaps, or a wrench that had bounced out of someone's pickup truck.

Bulging plastic bags dangled from the bicycle's rear fender, bags filled with half-squeezed tubes of oil paint – cadmium orange, yellow ochre, umber, alizarin crimson, viridian, aquamarine, titanium white – plus scraps of canvas and a handful of frazzled brushes. Although Snee had devoted four decades of his life to art, art had not reciprocated the favor.

"Yessiree," he sang out to a redwing blackbird perched on a nearby fencepost. "Informed sources agree, Tom Snee is the least-known artist at work in the world today."

Many times over the years Snee and his barrel had plunged over the edge of this, his own personal Niagara. Gallery owners dismissed his work with the casual arrogance of culture mavens who never for an instant doubted the superiority of their own aesthetic judgment – a criterion entirely dependent upon the cash register's tally.

"Too vibrant, too colorful," they said, or, "too much like Monet." And since few could afford a real Monet, the public bought countless cheap prints instead, prints still hanging and fading in every dentist's waiting room from Bennington to Island Pond.

As a result, the old Frenchman's heirs grew ever richer, while Snee grew ever thinner and as mad as a March hare.

His decline had been so gradual as to be imperceptible. Marginalized at first, then forgotten by his peers, his ostracism was total. The resulting stress took its toll. Frustration gave way to anger and then, as the collectors ignored his work and the museum curators all but laughed in his face, Snee's downward spiral gained momentum. Alcohol widened the gap between the world he once knew and the isolation he now endured.

No one knew how many canvases he'd hidden away in attics, basements and sheds. They moldered unseen and forgotten, fit only for the teeth of rodents or the eyes of art historians as yet unborn. As far as the art world was concerned, Snee was a scrap of human flotsam, nothing more than a shimmy in the electromagnetic spectrum, a glimmer between 480 and 640 Angstrom Units – an unsubstantiated rumor in three dimensions.

In an earlier era Snee would've been a hobo living near the railroad tracks in the grubby subculture called a hobo-jungle, populated by misfits, failures and those on the lam from one debilitating misfortune or another.

Snee may have been homeless, but he was not tentless.

Every summer he lived outdoors, camping secretly in the woods somewhere until the weather grew too cold or the indignant landowner stumbled upon his campsite and chased him off the property. No one knew or cared where he disappeared to in the winter. And so, the shabby artist inhabited a realm in which obsession and delusion played continuous double features on the drive-in movie screen of his mind. And although the concession stand remained open for business, Snee's demons had long since seized control of the projector, the focus knob and the popcorn.

Snee pushed his bicycle towards what the locals jokingly referred to as "bustling downtown Krampton." He walked past the church where the faithful gathered every Sunday for the expiation of their sins, but he doubted if anyone had ever managed to sin often or deeply enough to justify the weekly purge. Unlike the pious, Snee preferred to wait until his gullet was full before tickling the back of his throat with a spiritual feather.

Snee approached the general store and leaned his ancient Schwinn against an oak tree. He climbed three steps, pushed open the screen door and shuffled between shelves stocked with what the tourists considered to be quaint: Boxes of stale Rice Krispies, dusty cans of Spam, packets of expired Jell-O, spray cans of mosquito repellant, ammo and fishing tackle. Yard-long strips of sticky fly-tape hung in strategic corners to ensnare the unwary, many of which still buzz and kick with impotent fury.

The store's owner, Howard Burdock, sat behind the counter, deeply engrossed in either a newspaper, a lurid paperback thriller or a glossy magazine devoted to professional sports and slender young women in diminutive bathing suits. Gone were the days when a gaggle of flinty old geezers sat around a pot-bellied stove, hawking nicotine-enriched gobbets into a spittoon, eating Cross crackers and saying "ayup" from time to time. Instead, a television flickered quietly on a wall-mounted bracket, while oboes and violins droned interminably from Vermont Public Radio, interrupted by ever more frequent advertisements masquerading as funding attributions.

"What can I do you for today?" asked Howard, tearing his gaze from the image of a wasp-wasted wastrel in a thong bikini. A brawny six foot two, Howard's broad ursine face was fringed with a black beard, a lush pelt that gave him a resemblance to one of the carved wooden bears standing out front awaiting purchase.

"Gonna' do some impulsive buying," said Snee. "It's an all-American, two-fisted shopping spree."

"Go right ahead."

Snee knew exactly what he wanted – a Ring Ding and a can of black cherry soda. Unable to wean himself, he had gone from adolescence to addled senescence still scarfing down the chocolate-covered hockey pucks. He placed both items on the counter and looked around hesitantly.

"Anything else?"

"Maybe," said Snee as he perused the trinkets arrayed on the counter. A miniature leg-hold trap guaranteed to catch native Vermont mosquitoes caught his eye. Nearby stood a display featuring audiocassettes filled with Ferris Oxhide's folksy monologues about a way of life long gone, delivered in a Vermont dialect equally extinct.

The screen door opened and banged shut as two local roustabouts arrived. Hank and Zeke strode in wearing grimy overalls, baseball caps and knee-high rubber boots besmirched with used cow food. They smelled so bad the air around them seemed to ripple, charging the room with the high-octane stench of fresh manure – an indelible aroma notoriously resistant to hot water and soap.

"Gimme' one a' them sawsitches and a Slim-Jim and a Sky Bar," said Hank, pointing to a gallon jar filled with crimson cylinders floating in a mysterious liquid reputed to be formaldehyde. The sausages looked like something vile from a high-school biology lab – a donkey's penis perhaps – pickled for all eternity and studded with indigestible nodules of fat.

"There's nothing like a good lunch," said Zeke as he grabbed a box of powdered doughnuts and a six-pack of Bud Lite.

The screen door opened again and banged shut as Marion Witherspoon arrived. She nodded a greeting to Howard and turned to Hank. "Still working over to the Ticour Mill? And what about you, Zeke? Still tending Abe's herd?"

"Yes, maam. We're both still in harness."

A spry, gray-haired busybody in the absolute prime of her senility, Marion became the official Krampton town clerk after her husband passed away. She quickly revealed a talent for sticking her nose firmly into other people's business – much the way a Dalmatian will jam its bony snout into someone's crotch for a quick snuff to verify their gender.

"What's new, Marion?" said Howard. "Anything interesting happening in our little corner of the world? Any word yet as to when the water department intends to connect my camp to the municipal system?"

"It's going to cost you five thousand dollars," she answered, wasting no time in getting to the heart of the matter. "They'll have to dig a new line for a separate pipe from the pumping station to Lake Road. And before it can go forward you'll have to get everyone along the route to buy in."

"Hmmm," said Howard. "I was afraid of that. Maybe you can tell me why they built the system and ran the pipes to everyone except those of us nearest to the pump?"

"Couldn't say. Take it up at the next town board meeting."

"I'm getting awfully tired of having to haul my drinking water in gallon plastic jugs, week in and week out, summer and winter. The stuff that comes up from my well is the hardest, most pipe-corroding liquid you ever saw. It tastes bad and smells like rotten eggs. Hell, it kills houseplants and if you boil it, it turns purple!"

"I know all about it," she replied.

Howard and Marion stared at one another for a moment. Both were formidable disseminators of gossip. None could say which was Head Grape on the vine: Howard seemed to know everything that went on among the personal lives of the townsfolk, while Marion knew everything about their finances. "Speaking of water," she said, "have you seen Thad lately? His wife told me he went to the pumping station late yesterday afternoon, but she hasn't seen him since."

"No, he hasn't been in today. But I'll keep an eye out for him."

"I'm worried, Howard. It's not like him to wander off without leaving word."

"Maybe he went on a bender. He's probably in that strip club just over the Canadian border."

"Really, Howard, how can you say such a thing?"

Howard glanced at Snee and hollered, "Hey! Watch out."

The artist had taken a couple of steps back and now stood dangerously close to one of the hanging fly-strips. When the tape tickled his ear, he whirled around and succeeded in wrapping its length around his head.

"GET IT OFF!" he yelled, staggering and clawing at the tape as dozens of filth-bred bluebottles mashed against his face.

Marion frowned with annoyance as Howard rushed over and unwound the sticky strip from Snee's head.

"Crazy as a shit-house rat," said Hank, sniggering at the prospect of describing the event to his cronies at the paper mill.

"They ought to lock that buzzard up before he hurts himself," said Zeke.

"There you go," said Howard once he'd removed the tape. "You're all right."

Snee gathered up the tattered remains of his dignity, brushed the fly carcasses from his clothes and pointed to a roll of lottery tickets enshrined in a plastic display case.

"I'll tell 'ya what," he said. "I'll drop all charges in exchange for my snack and a couple of those 'Catch Champ' scratch-off lottery tickets."

Howard heaved a sigh of resignation. Then he walked behind the counter, tore a ticket from the roll and silently handed it over.

Snee fished a dime from the depths of his pants pocket and said, "Brother, can you spare a paradigm? But don't you fret, I'm gonna' use this dime to scratch off the winning numbers, not call my attorney."

Chapter Three

A shiny black SUV appeared in the distance. It approached, turned onto the dirt road alongside the Krampton Kountry store and sped by, raising a cloud of dust in its wake. Its destination – the boat access near the pump facility at Arnold Bay. The SUV bore smog-yellow Jersey plates and a freshman college student from Short Hills. Hitched to the bumper, a small trailer carried a gleaming Jet Ski with "THE ANNIHILATOR" splashed across its white plastic cowling in red letters that resembled crimson gouts of arterial blood. The driver's outlook on life was succinctly summed up by a decal that proclaimed "NO FEAR."

The SUV neared the water, swung around and backed slowly down the ramp until the trailer's wheels were submerged. The driver shifted into neutral and stepped down from the cab wearing orange baggies, a green T-shirt, blue-mirrored shades and an undernourished goatee. Gently lapping water caressed the inert Jet Ski as the young man waded into the water to detach the machine from its cradle. That completed, he parked the SUV and returned to straddle the Jet Ski. A push of a button roused it from slumber with a loud, aggressive snarl.

"This'll give the snail-darter, nature lovers something to think about," he mused as he twisted the throttle and zoomed away. His abrupt departure left behind a turbulent wake that slowly dispersed and a loud noise that did not. Still gaining speed, he traversed the bay and entered the broad lake. There, wind-driven waves and sheer momentum repeatedly hurled the machine clear of the surface for a split second, only to slam it back onto the surface with spine-jolting force.

Man and machine sped along on a course that took them past the small rock-rimmed island just south of the bay. The driver whooped and yelled as the Jet Ski carved tight aimless circles, shearing through the water like some mechanized water strider gone berserk – around and around – until, without warning, the engine sputtered and died.

The machine quickly lost all forward momentum and wallowed, as inert as a bar of Ivory soap in a bathtub. He pressed the starter button, but the engine only coughed.

"Come on, you expensive piece of crap, start!"

Repeated attempts flooded the engine.

And so, for the first time that day the young man sat still long enough to be able to observe his surroundings. He gazed at the mottled flanks of the Green Mountains rising in the east. Then he turned to look at the distant Adirondacks in the west, where filtered sunlight delineated the smoothly sculpted contours of the oldest mountains on the planet. Snake Mountain loomed to the south, rising unexpectedly from mid-lake like a vaporous blue mirage. Overhead, a jet that had taken off from Burlington International gained altitude and vanished into cumulus cloud.

The machine floated dead in the water, chilly waves splashed the driver's bare feet. Evaporation augmented by an incessant fifteen-mile-an-hour breeze chilled him still more, and when a cloud blotted out the sun, he decided he'd waited long enough.

"Enough nature," he declared. Once again he pushed the starter button, but the engine did not fire. Additional fruitless cranking reduced the battery's vitality, forcing him to sit and endure the enforced immobility.

* * *

Onshore, Tom Snee made his way to the lake. He abandoned his bicycle near the pebbled shore and ambled along the water's edge in search of a place to sit. The curved shoreline brought him to a large flat boulder, the perfect place to relax and scrape away the silver coating on his recently extorted lottery ticket. Snee extracted his lucky Harry S. Truman dime from a pocket, hoping against hope for a miraculous reversal of his fortunes. He was in no hurry and savored the fantasy of winning shared by all gamblers prior to rolling the dice, spinning the roulette wheel or betting on a horse.

Snee's reverie ended the instant he heard the Jet Ski's engine roar to life. He looked up and watched as it began to pick up speed. At a distance of 500 feet, the Jet Ski was too far away to see in any detail, but not too distant to prevent him from noticing something odd – the rider seemed to be kicking his legs as his mount veered erratically from side to side. After a minute the Jet Ski stabilized, then accelerated to its maximum velocity – shattering the silence and redlining the tachometer.

Snee forgot all about his lottery ticket as he watched the noisy contraption race towards the little island just south of the bay's entrance. The tortured engine sounded bad, clearly pushed beyond its limit. And as the Jet Ski rocketed across the surface, the prevailing breeze carried the unmistakable sound of a human scream, forming a dissonant harmony with the engine's own shriek.

Something was terribly wrong but all Snee could do was watch as the machine hurtled towards the island's rocky perimeter. It never turned, but instead caromed off the top of a submerged boulder and slammed into a narrow inlet between two steep cliffs. The machine ripped through the increasingly shallow inlet and struck the vertical rock wall at its inner terminus. A livid orange fireball billowed into the air and debris rained into the water.

There was no way Snee could've seen the impact, but the sound it created reached his ears a moment later – the ugly noise of plastic shattering, metal crumpling and bones splintering – a noise that would echo in his memory for a long time, to say nothing of the vicious WHUMP of an exploding gas tank. The wreckage of the machine and its owner burned furiously. Fed by plastic, gasoline, oil and flesh, a noxious smear of oily black smoke smudged the air. A revolting stench, had anyone been near enough to notice, was reminiscent of an outdoor barbeque that has gone horribly awry, as when the chef gets incinerated while squirting a can of charcoal lighter fluid on already glowing briquettes.

"Holy jumpin' Jesus H. Christ on a Pogo-Stick!" hollered Snee. "And I'll be jiggered if I know what the H stands for."

Hidden from his view, Snee didn't know whether or not the rider had jumped off the speeding contraption at the last moment. The afternoon tranquility reasserted itself as Snee watched the smoke rising above the island. He couldn't decide if he should notify the Coast Guard or the Navy. He pondered the question for a moment and then remembered his virgin lottery ticket. He began to scratch away the silver coating, and it didn't take long to reveal the results…

"Sorry. You are not a winner. Please try again."

Chapter Four

At five foot eight, State Police Sergeant Paul Edwards carried his endomorphic two hundred pounds with the fluid grace of a quarterback. Atop powerful shoulders welded to a barrel-chest, the sergeant's shaved head capped him much the way a 45-caliber cartridge is tipped with lead. The analogy ends there, however, as he possessed a keen analytical mind. With arms as thick as fence-posts and legs as strong as those that support a Steinway grand, he spent much of his free time lifting weights, karate-chopping bricks in half and splintering wooden planks with chest-high kicks.

Sergeant Edwards tilted his chair back, placed his feet up on the desk and stared at a litany of disaster displayed on the monitor of an aging computer. The database contained all the lake-related deaths that had occurred in the last 25 years – every drowning, boat collision, suicide jumper from the Champlain Bridge – plus the ice fishermen that broke through the ice out on the vast frozen expanse.

"It's enough to make a person move to Arizona," he decided. Sergeant Edwards swung his feet off the desk, opened a new file and entered the name of the latest casualty to the list – one Thaddeus Steady. A call had come in from the little town of Krampton in what at first looked like a simple case of a missing person. He'd driven out from police headquarters in Middlebury and talked to the victim's wife. Convinced that her concern was genuine, he'd searched the water pumping facility, only to discover a disarticulated skeleton lying amidst shredded clothing on the bottom of a cistern.

The bones had been gathered up and sent to the state forensic lab for analysis, but the results had not yet come in. Sergeant Edwards added details to the file but paused at the line labeled "Cause of Death." As if on cue, the fax machine awoke from its electronic slumber, scrolled out three pages and beeped. Edwards snatched them and began to read: "Using a gas spectrograph, the lab identified an organic poison in tissue samples taken from the remains – an extremely virulent nerve toxin originating from such an improbable source that, fearing error, we repeated the analysis three times, but the results never varied. The venom is remarkably similar to that produced by the Australian blue-ring octopus. Gouges and incisions on the bones were caused by species unknown."

This can't be right, thought the sergeant. In fact, it's preposterous. The blue-ring octopus lives twelve thousand miles away, on the opposite side of the planet. And how could the experts possibly fail to identify the species responsible? It made no sense.

The report went on:

"Producing one of the most potent poisons in nature, a bite from the blue ring is not required as mere contact with the cephalopod's skin can be fatal."

Edwards read the report with growing incredulity.

"According to Australian authorities – once bitten, the victim feels a tingling sensation around the lips and tightness in the chest, followed soon thereafter by the inability to speak. Paralysis sets in quickly and each breath becomes shallower than the one before. The victim remains fully conscious to the end."

"A pitiless little bastard," the sergeant concluded. He tossed the report onto his desk and imagined the scene on an Australian beach: The sunlight hammering down from a cloudless, blue sky as the surf hissed and boomed nearby. And there, lying inert on the sand, eyes wide – fixed and staring – the unfortunate victim hears his own epitaph, "This bloke's had it. He's dead."

The sergeant picked up the phone and dialed the state pathologist's office in Montpelier. It rang only once before someone answered. "This is Sergeant Edwards at State Police headquarters in Middlebury. Let me speak to Hendrik, please. Yes, I'll hold."

After a minute of vapid Muzak, a gruff voice barked, "Hendrik here."

"Hello H guy, this is Paul in Middlebury. I just read your report on the late Thaddeus Steady. The blue-ring octopus you say? Gouges on the bones caused by species unknown? What's going on over there in Montpeculiar, are you guys breathing toxic fumes or what?"

"Let me assure you, sergeant, we have entirely adequate ventilation in the lab. And yes, we identified the toxin as that of the blue-ring. Its venom has no antidote, incidentally. Other than that, we haven't a clue as to what dismembered the guy in Krampton. I performed the autopsy myself; I've never seen anything like it. The bones were stripped almost entirely clean of flesh, but the most intriguing detail concerns the tibias and femurs. They looked as if they'd been gouged with chisels."

"Tell me you're kidding."

"No. I never kid," said Hendrik, "especially when there's been an unexplained death. And I don't mind telling you, we had some difficulty identifying the toxin's molecular signature. Other than poison ivy, mosquitoes, ticks and a few rattlesnakes in the quarries near Fair Haven, there aren't any toxic organisms in Vermont. We were forced to expand our search radius, and eventually linked to a lab in Sydney."

"Australia?"

"That's right, and they identified it as belonging to the blue-ring. I spoke with their senior toxicologist for quite a while. Christ, you think we've got problems? Our most virulent venom is only a minor annoyance in comparison to those the Aussies have to deal with. Imagine an entire continent crawling with critters we've never heard of – many right in their own backyards – all just itching for a chance to bite or sting anyone or anything that gets in their way."

"That's all very interesting, Hendrik, but what does it have to do with us?"

"Hear me out, Paul, this is fascinating stuff. They've got this little green snake that has a particular fondness for backyard swimming pools, chlorine and all. If it bites you, the game's over. And that's just on dry land. Their indigenous marine life is twice as deadly and I'm not referring to all the crocodiles or sharks or stingrays that abound in their coastal waters. Forget vacationing in Australia."

"Good advice," said the sergeant, "but tell me, what have you done with Steady's remains?"

"Cremated."

"Already? That was quick. Your report left more questions than answers and you know how I hate unanswered questions."

"I do too, Paul, but we don't have the space to store everything that falls into our laps. The guy's widow wanted closure. Now she's got an urn full of ashes on her mantelpiece."

"Speaking of cremation, what can you tell me about the Jet Ski fatality?"

"Not much," said Hendrik. "The rider was smashed to a pulp and then burned to a crisp. We're assembling dental fragments for identification. Were there any witnesses?"

"Sort of. A crazy artist named Snee claims to have seen the Jet Ski zoom by just before the crash. But he was on the mainland and too far away to be of much help. Half of everything he said was gibberish, although he said the rider was screaming and kicking his legs just before impact."

"Build it and they will crash," said Hendrik. "Listen Paul, I've never heard of anyone running a Jet Ski into a rock wall at full speed. Sounds to me like a suicide – or should we say, 'jeticide?'"

The sergeant took a deep breath and frowned. "That makes two fatalities so far this season, both unexplained and both connected, in one way or another, to the lake."

"What did your team find at the site?"

"About what you'd expect. I went out on the police boat with the divers and we found wreckage and a greasy smudge on the rock cliff, caused by the fire. I spoke to the owner of the island, a guy named Stryker. He's a professor at the University of Vermont and lives on the island year-round. He heard the crash and called us."

"So," said Hendrik, "We've got one crispy-critter Jet-Ski suicide and a guy who was apparently killed by a tiny octopus that lives halfway around the globe. Not what I'd call a typical week in the North Country. The season hasn't even started yet but I've got a feeling it's going to be one hell of a summer."

"Christ, I hope you're wrong. Keep me posted."

Sergeant Edwards hung up, then turned his attention to the "Cause of Death" line in the database file and typed 'unknown.'

Chapter Five

Professor Stanley Stryker stood behind a rickety wooden lectern in the oldest lecture hall in the University of Vermont, a cavernous chamber long overdue for either restoration or demolition. He scrutinized his fledgling marine biology students as they climbed the steep amphitheater and wedged themselves into uncomfortable hundred-year old folding seats. The scene reminded him of the painting by Thomas Eakins, the one in which a group of 19th-century medical students listens with rapt attention as the Master dispenses Knowledge, while a partially dissected cadaver reposes before them on a slab.

Any similarity between the painting and the class disappeared when the professor cast his gaze about the upper tiers, watching through pale crocodilian eyes. His forehead rose steeply above a furrowed, craggy brow to meet a coiling thatch of silver hair as electric as the volatile filament in an old-fashioned flashbulb. The crease between his eyebrows deepened into a scowl.

"College students," he muttered; another batch of illiterate nitwits nurtured on MTV, rap music and graphic novels – a fidgeting throng of sexually active children.

The professor tapped his pointer stick on the side of the lectern. He waited until the commotion subsided, then began: "Charles Darwin's revolutionary – and evolutionary – theory evoked scorn when first published. Today, 150 years later, the debate still rages. Anyone care to hazard a guess as to why?"

All 137 seven students froze like so many nervous, wide-eyed impalas under the gaze of a hungry leopard. "You there, yes you," said the professor, pointing his stick at a music lover in the top row. A pair of earbuds came out and the student blushed crimson.

"Could you repeat the question?"

"Good of you to join us. I asked if anyone could tell us why the theory of evolution remains a hot-button issue, all these years later."

No one said a word.

The professor surveyed the class and shrugged.

"I'll tell you why the Creationists still wrestle with the Darwinians. The 'Old Man' himself answered this question in the introduction to his book,

'*The Origin of Species.*' It's quite simple, actually. The controversy persists with undiminished ferocity due to Man's inability to grasp the sheer immensity of time required to produce life on our planet. Add to that the equally inconceivable span of time necessary to evolve the countless permutations we see alive today and in the fossil record. The lifespan of a human being is the merest blink of the eye when compared to the hundreds of millions of years the Earth has whirled through space in its orbit around the sun."

The students took notes using pencils, pens and laptop computers. In one instance a tiny tape recorder caught his every word, and it was to this electronic eavesdropper that he addressed his next remark.

"In other words, my glossy young chimps, you are simply not intelligent enough to be able to grasp the depths of Time, so you might as well accept that fact right now!"

The sharp crack of his pointer stick hitting the lectern emphasized the point. The students glanced at one another nervously, much the way sailors embarking on a three-year voyage might react upon first encountering Bligh, their new captain.

"Here's another interesting brain teaser," said the professor in an amiable tone of voice, as if employing good teacher/bad teacher tactics borrowed from the cops. "Why did the turtles, snakes, crocodiles and other reptiles survive while the dinosaurs perished?"

A hand waved in the air.

"Yes, and your name is…?"

"Ms. Bryan. The dinosaurs died because they weren't allowed on Noah's ark."

A sudden hush descended upon the hall.

"The ark you say? Tell us where you gleaned this pearl of wisdom."

"The Bible is clear as to where the animals came from and when God put people upon the Earth: The Lord made everything in six days, four thousand years ago."

The professor heaved a sigh of disgust and said, "Let me remind you, Ms. Bryan, the study of mythology is done on the other side of the campus, a very long way round the bend."

A flurry of snickers rippled through the hall.

Another hand fluttered aloft. "What about intelligent design?"

"I do not allow superstition to intrude upon my science class. Although here again, the incremental evolutionary advances – the dazzling array of complexity and bio-diversity – occurred over such an unimaginable expanse of time that we humble simians are ill equipped to grapple with, let alone comprehend, such enormity. Now, if there are no further questions, we'll move on.

"The dinosaurs dominated our planet for 100 million years. Try to wrap your diminutive brains around that! One hundred million years is a span of time 100 times greater than the entire existence of Man as a species. We know this because we have irrefutable fossil evidence and a very reliable way to date these fragments of once-living creatures. And yet, the turtle still lives and thrives, a creature that gives every indication of having completed its evolutionary development."

A hand waved in the front row, the position traditionally occupied by "A" students.

"What do you think of all the recent 'Champ' sightings? Could there really be something swimming around in Lake Champlain that was thought to be extinct?"

"First of all, there would have to be more than one, as it takes two to tango. And if a pair of Champosaurs did exist, the most likely candidate would be the reptile known as a plesiosaur. Plesiosaur is Greek for 'nearer to a lizard.' We've all seen the painted renditions – the bronto-shaped body with a long neck, paddle-shaped fins and a lengthy tail. We know from fossils that there were hundreds of species of plesiosaur. The remains of entire specimens have been found, complete down to the smallest bone in their tails and a bellyful of gastroliths – the small round stones in the creature's stomach used to help grind their food. But to answer your question, I strongly doubt such a possibility, for the simple reason that a large carnivorous reptile could not withstand a Vermont winter."

The "A" student posed another question. "Wouldn't an aquatic creature have a better chance of surviving whatever it was that caused the mass extinction?"

"Good point, but the answer is no – which brings us to the question: What caused the extinction of the dinosaurs 65 million years ago? For many years the 'Gradualists' fought the 'Catastrophists' over this issue. The 'Gradualists' believed in the theory of Racial Senescence, a theory that claims the dinosaurs perished because they had developed overspecialized physical traits, traits that impeded or prevented the modifications necessary for survival."

Professor Stryker clicked a remote and projected the image of an immense flaming meteor entering the Earth's atmosphere.

"Imagine a meteor with a diameter of six miles and a trajectory that resulted in a collision with the Earth. The meteor struck a cataclysmic blow equal to thousands of nuclear bombs going off all at once. The explosion threw an immense cloud of iridium-bearing dust into the atmosphere – a cloud that encircled the globe and drastically reduced the amount of sunlight reaching the surface, creating an 'impact winter.' A pre-meteorite theory spoke of gradual climate change, but thanks to Louis Alvarez and his son's discovery of the iridium layer in the earth's crust, the 'Catastrophists' have carried the day. Iridium is a rare element on Earth, but plentiful in meteors.

"After this cataclysmic strike, the sea became acidified – killing all plankton – and so, starting at the very bottom, entire food chains were wiped out. All photosynthesis stopped. Plant-life quickly ceased. The herbivores succumbed, as did the carnivores that preyed upon them.

"Of course, the iridium theory was just that – a theory – until the Space Shuttle photographed the remains of a crater in the Yucatan Peninsula. Geological forces, combined with vegetation, obscured the crater from all eyes on the ground; but there it is, a crater six miles wide, formed 65 million years ago."

The professor clicked the remote again and projected a view of the Earth from space, a perspective from which the crater's circumference was clearly visible.

As the lecture droned on for another 40 minutes, the squirming in the narrow wooden seats gradually increased. Aware of the growing restlessness, the professor concluded by saying, "I'd like you to think about why the crocodiles managed to survive while the dinosaurs perished. Crocs have been around for a very long time. Was it an accident? Or did they owe their survival to a lack of specialization?" A loud buzz from the clock above the door signaled the end of the lecture.

"That's it for today. I'll expect you to have read chapters one through four in book one of Hardisty for next time. This may seem like a heavy assignment for so early in the semester, and it is, but we have a lot of ground to cover."

Laptops snapped shut and the miniature tape recorder clicked off. Pens, pencils and notebooks vanished into knapsacks and a dozen pairs of earbuds were quickly inserted. The folding desktops were pushed aside as 137 students rose to their feet and clattered down the amphitheater's steep wooden steps. The mob surged through the hall, burst out the main door and into the afternoon rain.

Chapter Six

After a seemingly endless succession of overcast days, the monotonous gray ceiling above the state grew frayed and tattered. Gaps of startling blue appeared and slowly expanded. When the sun finally emerged between the clouds it cast swiftly moving shadows across the land. Steel tines turned up umber clods of fertile soil as a tractor crept across the field bordered by Lake Road. A flock of seagulls clambered in its wake, snapping up the freshly exposed grubs and black beetles as they scurried for cover. When the tractor reached the perimeter it turned 180 degrees and cut a new swathe, driving the gulls aloft in a squawking, wheeling throng.

A mauve minivan with New York plates traversed the narrow lane. The driver pulled over at a gap in a dense thicket of scrub and cedar. After stepping out and flexing knees stiff from hours of immobility, he unlocked a padlock and swung open the gate guarding the entrance to his property.

Little did he know he was being watched from behind a hedge, 50 feet away.

At 62, Harvey was tall and lean and looked like a suburban Gary Cooper. He ran a hand through black hair, combed straight back and lacquered in place by the pomade once reviled as "greasy kid stuff."

Dot, his frail blonde wife, slowly emerged from the passenger side. She opened the cargo door and clasped a cane in one hand and three dog leashes in the other. Her trio of Springer Spaniels stretched, jumped out and tugged at their restraints, eager to empty their bladders and reacquaint themselves with the great outdoors. Dot leaned against the van, exhausted by the long drive up from their winter home in Armonk.

"There goes the neighborhood," muttered Snee from behind the bushes.

Harvey and Dot walked across a lawn in dire need of mowing and approached their tightly shuttered summerhouse, one slow measured step at a time. Dot held onto the leashes while Harvey unscrewed a plywood batten, unlocked a glass door and slid it open. He was all too aware of a fourth leash gripped firmly in his wife's bony fist – an invisible choke chain around his own throat – a restraint that became uncomfortable only when he attempted to resist her indomitable will.

The dogs surged into the dark interior, dragging their mistress across the threshold. They wrenched free and bounded, yipping and yapping into the far corners of the dark, shuttered house.

Dot loved Sam, Cricket and Max with a fervor that only a childless woman could lavish upon such shaggy and irascible surrogates. And although Harvey was equally devoted, he thought of them as Hoover, Kirby and Electrolux.

* * *

Still watching from behind the hedge, Snee retreated stealthily. He carelessly ditched his bicycle in a robust patch of poison ivy and crept through a stand of gnarled cedars, then over the crest of a plateau and down the precipitous slope leading to the water's edge.

Suddenly a partridge exploded into the air and damn near gave him a heart attack. The bird rocketed away through the branches on a blur of stubby wings. Snee froze till the hammering in his chest subsided. Then he continued on until he came to a level patch of ground. There, protected by an escarpment of rock at his back and cedars on either side, Snee's illicit campsite commanded a million dollar view of the lake and Adirondacks. Although the summerhouse stood only a few hundred feet away, beyond the crest of the hill, Snee had chosen his campsite well and thought it unlikely the landowners would ever find him.

Overhead, a pair of red squirrels chased one another around a cedar trunk. They spotted the trespasser and abruptly ceased pursuit.

"Why do the heathen rage?" Snee asked the rodents as they flicked their tails and chittered indignantly. "It's those blue-nosed, pencil-necked, Puritan sons 'a bitches! They'll pay a pauper's ransom for a lapdog computer and in a few years it'll be in the junk-heap. But will they buy a painting – a thing of beauty that will last forever? No!"

He paused for a breath. "Well, they can keep their summer homes and their sports utility dump trucks and their sour grapes too, for all I care!"

* * *

"Harvey! These dogs are driving me crazy! Round them up and hand me their leashes!" Harvey obeyed, but all three spaniels dashed in a circle, entwining and trussing her in a bundle.

"Harvey! Do something!"

"It okay, Dot. Relax. They're just excited."

She glared at him as he unwound the leashes. "Get the plywood off the windows, it's like a mausoleum in here."

"One thing at a time, Dot."

Once freed, the animals sprang away, eager for more fun. "I'd like to shoot all the damn dogs right now," she said in exasperation. "My pistol is around here somewhere."

"Okay Dot, you do that," said Harvey, knowing the Walther was still safely packed away in the van. He'd bought the weapon after succumbing to the fallacious belief that owning one would increase their security, especially during sojourns in the comparative solitude of Vermont. While Dot feared a burglar, Harvey's paranoia was racially motivated, based upon what he perceived as the threat from the perennially lawless members of society, "those goddamn jungle bunnies."

"I'm going to turn the water on," he said. "Before I unload the van."

Dot collapsed into a recliner's soft embrace and said, "Plug in the television first and get me a drink. I don't care what the doctor said."

"Okay Dot, but tomorrow, when you're wiped out, just remember it's the price for ignoring his advice." Harvey brought in the cardboard box containing the liquor and mixed her a screwdriver. "Here you go, knock yourself out."

Dot swallowed half the drink and said, "Now the TV." As the vodka entered her bloodstream, she recalled the day twelve years earlier when her doctor said, "You have multiple sclerosis. Your myelin sheaths – the wrappings that surround your nerve fibers – are slowly being destroyed by your own immune system. I'm very sorry but there's nothing we can do to stop it."

Harvey walked outside, crossed the spacious yard and unlocked the door to his meticulously restored, two hundred year old barn. Its exterior walls had weathered silver and not for one moment did he consider the 12-foot satellite dish mounted on its roof to be incongruous. On the contrary, the device was essential. Television provided Dot with her only link to the outside world – even though her viewing habits embraced little except soap operas, crime dramas and the Shopping Channel.

Harvey opened the breaker panel inside the barn and switched on the electricity, then returned to the house.

"Harvey, the water's still off."

"Hmmm . . . I'll have to go down and check the pump."

Toolbox in hand, he walked around the house and skirted the in-ground swimming pool that lay within a perimeter of grass bordered by fir trees. Harvey had given up draining the pool in the fall, having found it easier and less time consuming to scoop out the dead leaves in the spring. And so, the water froze every winter, thawed in the spring and required regular maintenance throughout the summer. Numerous frogs leapt into the pool at his approach. He ignored them and followed a path through the woods that brought him to a shed built on an exposed promontory 30 feet above the lake. From there, a plastic hose snaked down the rock face and disappeared below the water's surface.

Harvey opened the shed and checked the main valve to make sure it was open. The motor whined laboriously and he realized the intake must be clogged. No sense in burning out the pump, he decided, and shut it off. He descended a flight of rusty metal steps to the concrete block that lay partially submerged at the water's edge.

Water lapped at the rocks – many covered with mossy green filaments that undulated in the ebb and flow like a swimmer's hair. Other rocks were covered by colonies of zebra mussels, each brown and white striped shell no larger than a fingernail, but each as sharp as a scalpel.

Harvey stepped onto a flat rock amidst the scree – fractured basalt – the result of dynamite used to reshape the cliff prior to the installation of the steps. He paused to relish the aroma of fresh water and algae.

"Just as I thought," he muttered after pulling the heavy black tubing out of the water. The metal nozzle was encased with zebra mussels.

Harvey shifted his weight and the rock tipped beneath him, throwing him off balance. He plunged forward into the water, raking both hands against thick encrustations of zebra mussels. He rose to his knees cursing, staggered out of the water and stood dripping on the concrete block.

It all happened so quickly that at first he was unaware of the deep incisions in his palms. Anesthetized by the cold water, the pain quickly blossomed and he stared at the highly oxygenated blood dripping from his hands. Harvey felt slightly nauseous as he held both arms over his head to slow the bleeding.

Wounded or not, he knew the water problem had to be resolved. And so, using just the tips of his fingers, he gingerly grasped the tubing and used an adjustable wrench to remove the clogged nozzle. Then he flung the open-ended hose back into the water, climbed the steps and switched the pump back on. This time the motor whirred smoothly as water flowed unimpeded from the lake to the house.

Harvey had only two things on his mind as he walked along the path, demarcating his route with crimson spots… a first-aid kit and a stiff drink.

Chapter Seven

The lake lay as smooth and reflective as a mirror, its pellucid surface dappled by only the faintest paw-print of moving air. A battered old Dodge pickup came to a halt alongside the boat ramp. Abe, the vehicle's equally antique driver, opened the passenger's door and said, "Out you go, Rocky, you know the drill." The aging collie with the soft wheezing woof ambled to the ground and began to sniff amongst the detritus, searching for the lingering aromas that give meaning to a dog's life.

Man, collie and truck had shared many miles. Given enough whiskey, dog-chow and an oil change now and then, all three might last a while yet. Nowadays though, Abe's eyesight was bad, the engine burned oil and when Rocky barked, the chipmunks just laughed.

Countless blue stones covered the beach, each one worn smooth and round by centuries of abrasion. Those at the waterline were the size of dimes; a foot inland they grew to silver dollars and then to saucers. Many bore calcium striations – illegible white zigzags as if autographed by God himself. Abe bent down and picked up a perfect skimming stone, drew back his arm and threw – a ritual he'd performed since boyhood. The stone hit the surface and skipped – again and again and again – until it lost momentum and sank to the bottom.

The old dairyman contemplated the stones still lying at his feet. After flinging them for decades, he wondered why there didn't seem to be any missing.

Abe hauled an aluminum canoe off the truck and dragged it to the water's edge. He stowed his fishing tackle, a paddle, and then eased the canoe into the water, pushing until the metal bottom no longer scraped against the submerged rocks. Rocky stepped over the gunwale and took his customary position at the bow. Then, with one last shove, Abe jumped in and the canoe glided smoothly away.

The old man propelled the canoe forward with strength that belied his 74 years. Each paddle stroke created a miniature whirlpool that receded in the pale green surface waters.

Abe felt pretty good, all things considered, and he welcomed the new life emerging from countless fonts – the recently hatched snakes that surveyed the world for the first time, the young rabbits and groundhogs and foxes –

even the black fly and mosquito larva that squirmed prior to bolstering an invincible armada of their bloodthirsty brethren.

Abe looked at the sky – robin's egg blue at the horizon, a deep aquamarine at the zenith. The Adirondacks loomed to the west, tier upon tier of serrated ridgelines receding into azure haze – their contours scoured by wind, water and erosion. Maybe that's how old age works, he mused, constant erosion till there's nothing left.

Abe knew every trick in the book for outwitting and catching his wily, finned adversaries, but lately neither lures nor worms did the trick. The fish simply weren't biting.

"Think we'll catch anything today?" he asked the dog.

Rocky grinned.

"What do you know? Solid bone from ear to ear."

Abe picked up his fishing rod, held the monofilament with an index finger, opened the bail and cast. The silver spoon glinted in midair, then landed 40 feet away with a soft kerplunk! He allowed it to sink and then began to reel in, varying the pace, making the lure twist and flash in the dim green water like the silver belly of a minnow.

The lure attracted the attention of a lake trout.

Although it had recently dined on a fresh hatch of Mayflies, it couldn't afford to ignore the prospect of another meal. The trout rounded on the lure and struck.

Abe felt the tug, flexed the rod and sank the barbed hook into the fish's jaw.

The trout swerved sharply and fought against the invisible force pulling it to the surface, but there was no escape. Once netted, Abe placed the iridescent speckled creature gently on the bottom of the canoe, where it quivered, its mouth open, eyes staring.

After moistening his hands, Abe grasped the fish firmly, and with the aid of a pair of needle-nose pliers, he carefully removed the hook from its jaw. Only then did he notice the parasite attached to the trout's belly. A slender young lamprey peered at him through tiny black eyes. Abe pressed his knife-blade below the lamprey's sucker-disk and pried it off, revealing a circular wound where the predator had rasped away the scales.

Abe lowered the trout into the lake and released his grasp. The stunned fish lingered at the surface just long enough to realize it was free, and then, with an abrupt splash, vanished into the cold viridian depths.

"Today is that fish's lucky day," Abe informed the dog. Then he picked up the lamprey by the tail and whacked its head against the side of the canoe, killing it instantly. He tossed the limp corpse to Rocky, who caught it in midair and swallowed it whole.

"What a disgusting snack," said Abe.

The fisherman turned his gaze to the east, to the silver-domed silo rising above the trees half a mile away. Split-Rock farm had been his entire life, and his father's before him, but now, as age weighed ever more heavily, Abe supervised the day-to-day operation but gratefully relinquished the never-ending hard work to his hired hands, Hank and Zeke.

* * *

Hank and Zeke were, at that very moment, entering Abe's barn; a cavernous wooden structure that enveloped them like a warm, moist stomach. Dangling light bulbs offset the gloom, but the smell hit each man like a punch in the nose. Pigeons perched overhead on rafters, bobbing their heads, cooing and spattering the ground with bacteria-laden ejecta.

"It's Friday, again," said Hank as they trudged through an ankle-deep mash of mud, urine and manure. "Another week shot to hell. When I finish work, I'm gonna' take a shower, grab some leftover pizza and then knock back a few cold ones."

The two men shoveled in silence as cluster-flies congregated on the cow's eyelids to sip moisture like some fiendish demimonde quaffing espresso.

"Gawddamit," said Zeke as a cluster-fly wedged into his left nostril, forcing him to expel the nasty intruder with a snort. "That sounds 'bout right. What else is there to do around here except work, drink beer or stick a shotgun barrel in your mouth? Tomorrow I'm goin' fishin,' even if it's raining like racehorses pissing. Wanna' come? We probably won't catch anything, you know how shitty it's been lately, but the Fishin' Derby's gettin' closer every day and we should be out there."

"Jeezus, Zeke. Tell me something I don't know already," said Hank peevishly.

"Okay, how 'bout this . . . They just announced this year's grand prize: A 24-foot Bayliner, complete with trailer and a full tank of gas."

Hank stopped dead in his tracks.

"Twenty-four feet?" The gleaming vessel floated in the stagnant lagoon of his imagination – all he had ever wanted and would probably never attain, in spite of his unstinting efforts to win the Fishing Derby every year.

"Yup. And the gas alone is worth hundreds of dollars. Tell me something, Hank. How much money do 'ya think we poured into the Derby over the years? Ever stop to add it all up? After all this time, I say we deserve to win that friggin' contest."

There was no denying it. Ever since the derby's inception, the desire to own such a boat had driven them to each fork over the annual $50.00 entry fee. And every year they sat in a shabby, wooden rowboat watching luxury cabin cruisers surge past, each one equipped with depth finders and bikini-clad babes draped languorously on chaise-lounges. Hank and Zeke stared as the women anointed each other with suntan lotion. Sometimes the cruiser goddesses waved as they glided by. Sometimes Hank and Zeke waved back.

Lost in thought, the two men shoveled fresh, steaming manure. Although neither man could see the cows huddling in their holding pen, they heard loud, flatulent outbursts each time one emptied its bowels.

Once they'd finished mucking out the stalls, Hank started up a small tractor and plowed the offal into the three-sided bunker that stood beyond the barn's northern wall. Tarps held down by bald tires covered the manure as it slowly grew from mound to mountain. Not far away a stream emerged from a pine forest – a brook that fed a pond as well as the herd's drinking trough, inside the barn.

Six ducks floated on the pond's smooth surface. Busily preening their feathers and nuzzling the silt for edible morsels, they were, in every sense of the term, sitting ducks.

A large snapping turtle lurked unseen beneath them.

The ducks paddled nervously towards the pond's far corner as Hank's manure tractor rolled closer. Suddenly the snapper seized a duck's webbed foot in its jaws and wrenched it under. One moment it was there – healthy, happy, feathers iridescent in the sunlight – the next moment gone!

The other ducks squawked bloody murder and scattered, flapping frantically and producing concentric ripples that expanded across the surface. Hank watched them gain altitude and fly off, then parked the tractor and dismounted – his head filled with thoughts of roast duckling glazed with sweet and sour sauce.

The inexplicable clamor of a herd in distress erupted within the barn. Loud, frenzied mooing and bleating accompanied the racket of hooves kicking the wooden walls.

Zeke dashed out and yelled, "Run! They've lost their friggin' minds!"

Planks bulged and splintered and out galloped a torrent of cows, each one hell-bent on getting as far away from the barn as possible. Both men sprinted towards the tractor and clambered up and onto the engine cowling. An instant later all 38 cows thundered by like so many wildebeests on the

Serengeti. Once beyond the barnyard, the herd turned onto the road and charged off in both directions.

"What in blue blazes happened in there?" asked Hank.

"I dunno," said Zeke. "They were drinkin' at the trough, just like always. All of a sudden they went ape-shit like hornets was stingin' 'em. I never saw nothin' like it."

* * *

A quarter mile away Marion Witherspoon glanced up from the town's fiscal report in time to see a herd of cows galloping down the driveway towards her. As the beasts drew near they slowed to a trot, and then a walk, before shuffling onto the spacious wooden deck that extended beyond her kitchen door.

"Oh dear," she quavered as the animals crowded onto the deck. Now enclosed by a stout wooden railing, the cows regained their composure and proceeded to tip over and trample her beloved collection of jade trees, spider plants and African violets. The cows nuzzled the hanging birdfeeders, then tipped and spilled thousands of sunflower seeds.

"Scat!" she ordered.

The cows ignored her.

"Vamoose! … Amscray!… Skidaddle!"

Still no response.

The terms had always worked before with dogs, cats and grandchildren. What was the correct word for dispersing cows, she wondered?

The cow standing nearest raised its head and looked through the screen door and into Marion's tidy kitchen. "Oh no you don't," she said and slammed the stout inner door.

Chapter Eight

The following morning brought more rain. At six-thirty the roads were empty – too early for the summer tourists to be anywhere but asleep in motel beds or in silver motor homes the size of a Soyuz-7 spacecraft. The big-rig drivers were up, however, seated in the diner just south of Krampton – guzzling coffee and devouring platters of bacon, eggs and home fries, better known as a "cholesterol slam." You could tell by looking at their creased, leathery faces they were dying to light that first cigarette after breakfast, and then, squinting from beneath the brim of a baseball cap, climb into their rigs and rumble across the Champlain Bridge, on into deepest, darkest New York state.

Tires hissed on wet pavement as a Vermont Fish and Wildlife truck moved through the early morning rain. Two state Wildlife officers wore dark green shirts with embroidered patches that proclaimed "Freedom and Unity" in terse Yankee brevity. The agency's devotion to iconography reached its peak on the vehicle's side doors; the state seal featured a tree, a cow and a deer – waiting, presumably, to be felled, milked or shot.

Thwack!

The truck's left front tire mashed a fat green frog into a slimy red pancake.

"Look's like frog poppin' time again," said Walter, the driver.

Thwack! Another frog flattened. Hundreds of them sat on the road – some healthy and robust, others just plain busted. Soon, crows would swoop down and scrape up the morsels with their beaks.

The younger man riding shotgun said, "Can't you steer around them?"

"I share your concern for livings things," said Walter, "but if I concentrated on avoiding every blessed frog in the road, I wouldn't be watching where I was going, now would I?"

Thwack!

"There's just too many. No way to avoid them."

The day had begun muggy and would only get worse as the temperature climbed. Low, moisture-laden clouds obscured the hills and only a smudge of lighter gray marked the sun's presence.

"Tell me, Walter, what do you make of the frogs found with three legs or with none at all?"

"I'd say something was definitely out of kilter."

"Yes, I agree. But I'm beginning to suspect the deformities could be our fault," said George. "Maybe the frogs are giving us a warning; you know, like the canaries used in mines to detect toxic gas. Maybe we should be trying to figure out what's wrong instead of poisoning the streams."

"Let me tell you something," Walter replied. "You're new to the department and maybe you don't quite realize what's at stake here – it's money, plain and simple. Think of all the folks who come to Vermont every summer for their vacations; they spend a ton of cash on food, gas and motels so they can run their boats on Lake Champlain and catch a decent fish or two. Without our intervention the state's tourist economy would go belly up in a big hurry."

"I understand," said George, "but what if the stuff we're pouring into the streams isn't as selective as we think? Maybe we're meddling with Mother Nature and causing more harm than good."

"We're Fish and Wildlife officers, for crying out loud, it's our job to meddle with nature! The stuff we use kills only the larva, while they're still harmless," Walter replied.

"That's not possible, Walter. There's no such thing as a selective pesticide. Didn't we learn anything from the DDT disaster back in the 'fifties, when we almost wiped out the eagles? I'm convinced we've upset a delicate natural balance. The deformed frogs are just the beginning."

Thwack!

Walter shifted down into third as the truck approached a gap in the wall of trees. They turned left onto a narrow dirt road and continued beneath an overarching green tunnel of dripping leaves.

"How many streams are we supposed to treat today?" asked George. "And how many more is it going to take?"

"Initially, it started as a 5-year plan: We dose the tributaries every spring, but lately the word's come down from Montpelier – we do it every year from now on."

"What, forever?"

"That's right. If the program is halted, the parasites would win and the local economy would lose. And in case you've forgotten, we're paid to do what the politicians in charge tell us to do. If you don't like it you can always quit, but as for me, the sooner we kill every last lamprey, the better."

Normally, the stream designated 117-E on their map was a shallow, rocky tributary. But as a result of the rain, it was now a wide, rushing torrent. The truck pulled over and the two wildlife officers unloaded a 30-gallon drum and rolled it to the edge of the stream. George attached a transparent plastic hose and opened the valve, releasing an unnaturally bright yellow liquid called Zentiloft. The chemical merged into the current, quickly diffusing into an ever more dilute state as it flowed over and around a multitude of rocks and boulders.

"Zentiloft damages the larva's pituitary gland and prevents them from maturing," said Walter. "Now all we have to do is check the weirs downstream and collect any lamprey that may have been caught. I'll do it. It should only take a few minutes."

Walter set off carrying a plastic bucket as George watched the yellow liquid pour from the hose. Every species that lived in the water would soon taste the chemical's bitter tang – the protozoa, copepods, newts, tadpoles, frogs, mudpuppies, turtles and fish. And as the lampricide slowly migrated up the food chain, it grew ever more concentrated. Osprey would eventually get their share, after eating the fish they impaled with their talons. It was just a matter of time before traces wound up in a frying pan – a fish fillet sautéed in butter and fed to a child.

Walter walked along the edge of the stream, stepping carefully on slippery stones the size of cantaloupes. The rain tapered off and stopped, although fitful breezes shook fat droplets from the trees. When the stream curved to the right the senior Wildlife officer disappeared from view behind a green partition of vegetation.

After another hundred feet he came to a swatch of red paint on a tree trunk, the signal indicating the weir's proximity. Unlike Native American weirs, this one was small, designed to catch only a limited number of lamprey – just enough for dissection and analysis, not for consumption.

When the last drops of Zentiloft had drained away, George rolled the empty drum back to the truck and stowed it. He sat in the cab, switched on the radio and waited. Several classic rock tunes later he grew impatient, glanced at his watch and decided he'd waited long enough. George stepped out, cupped his hands and hollered, "Hey Walter! Hurry it up!"

The shout went unanswered.

He set off, grumbling, to find his associate and followed the margins of the stream until he came to the tree with the red swatch. There, he turned and saw Walter lying facedown in the shallows amidst a group of boulders. Convinced the older man had suffered a heart attack, he rushed into the shin-deep water and grasped his shoulders, rolled him over and pulled him up into a sitting position.

The naked white bone of a skull grinned obscenely where Walter's face should've been. The flesh was gone, stripped away – eye sockets empty – one eyeball dangling like a half-eaten hard-boiled egg. George recoiled with horror and fell backward. Walter's body toppled sideways as George scrabbled away on elbows and heels, kicking at the stones until he slid into a deeper pool up to his waist. The water immediately began to seethe and churn. The green fabric of his pants bulged and tore apart as he went under, still kicking and thrashing. Water abruptly choked off the sound of his scream, although it remained loud in his own ears until all breath had been expended.

Chapter Nine

Marion Witherspoon marched into the Krampton Kountry store, faced Howard across the counter and said, "What on earth is going on around here? Do you know? Does anyone know? I've heard stories lately that would curl your hair."

"Hello Marion. You seem to have an unusually large bee in your bonnet today. What exactly are you referring to?"

"Well, there's Thad's death, the Jet-Ski incident, cows going crazy – running wild and destroying my plants – that sort of thing. And, I happen to know that the State Police had to carry Thad's body out, or what was left of it, in a plastic bag!"

"What do you mean 'what was left?'"

"Bits and pieces."

"I heard he drowned."

"That's the official story. The police are keeping a tight lid on what really happened, but I have my spies."

"Marion, I wouldn't pay too much attention to rumors. Freak accidents happen all the time and it's an unfortunate coincidence this one happened so close to home."

"Accidents, you say? What about Abe's cows breaking out of the barn and stampeding? Cows don't have accidents, Howard. I tell you, those animals were scared silly. I can't put my finger on it, but there's something mighty peculiar going on. Call it woman's intuition, but I know something's dreadfully wrong." Before she could continue, the radio scanner on a nearby shelf squawked.

Howard leaned over and listened to a police broadcast punctuated by bursts of static.

"There have been two more deaths," he said. "A couple of Fish and Wildlife officers have been found slain in the woods near Rock Cove, possibly murdered."

"What did I tell you," said Marion. "Thing's around here are going to hell in a hand-basket. The newspaper will splash this across the front page for a week. The TV people will swarm like vultures and Krampton will become the center ring of a media circus. Mark my words, Howard, this will scare off the tourists."

"Let's not jump to conclusions, Marion. We don't yet know anything about what happened. It's too soon to worry about the tourists; although I must admit, business has been slow. The weather's been so fickle I haven't sold a fishing license all week. I expect things will pick up once the Fishing Derby starts, it always does. As for this new trouble, it'll dominate tomorrow's headlines, but in a day or two there'll be some new disaster somewhere and people will forget all about us."

"No one's ever been murdered in Krampton before," said Marion. "Do you think that radio message was someone's idea of a sick joke?"

"No, I'm afraid it sounded all too real."

Just then the screen door opened and in walked Snee looking like Johnny Appleseed meets Albrecht Durer. Thin, frayed and grubby, all that was missing was a dented saucepan on his head.

"Salutations," he said, sweeping the air with his arms in a broad flourish. "Bartender! Give me a bladder of titanium white. And I don't mean a tube of Ipana for a blinding smile either."

"Sorry, we don't carry art supplies."

"Why not?"

"Not enough demand."

"I demand a tube of titanium white!"

"It doesn't work that way."

Howard was about to explain the concept of supply and demand when he became aware of a sound rarely heard in Krampton. A police siren sliced the air – faint at first but growing louder by the second, followed by the equally rare sight of a speeding State Police cruiser. All three watched through the store's plate glass window as it swept around the curve out front – blue lights flashing, tires squealing, pebbles flying, dust billowing.

"He's heading to Rock Cove," said Howard. "That radio bulletin certainly got his attention. Proves it wasn't a hoax."

Chapter Ten

"Bloody hell," muttered Roland Humphrey from behind the wheel of his Jaguar XK-E. An approaching rust-bucket Chevy had turned broadside into his lane and stalled. Roland's first impulse was to press the red button on the stick of his Spitfire Mark IV and give the offender a squirt from all eight cannons. But he was not flying a 'Spit, nor was the Chevy a bogey at twelve o'clock. Instead, he downshifted and steered the Jag nimbly around. The Abarth exhaust pipes emitted a throaty roar reminiscent of a Spitfire's Merlin engine – one last roar from the British Empire's aged lion.

The roadster hugged the curves as the lane skirted the contours of the lake. The convertible zoomed past a dilapidated farmhouse sagging under the weight of time and neglect. A dog chained to a tree scribed a dusty brown circumference in the dirt. A rusted satellite dish bloomed in the unkempt yard like an alien flower amidst the debris of broken lawn mowers, shattered lawn furniture and expired snowmobiles.

"No indoor plumbing, I suspect, but 200 channels on the telly," said the young woman seated beside Roland. "According to the map, Rock Cove Resort is another five miles. We're almost there."

The former RAF pilot and his granddaughter crossed the Krampton town line and continued on to the store. Roland pulled over and said, "I'm going to nip in for a quick chat. Maybe the proprietor can direct us to a marina. Care for anything? A Schwepps Bitter Lemon, perhaps?"

"No thanks, I'm fine," said Jade.

The XK-E and Roland's granddaughter created a remarkably photogenic sight – both, in Roland's eyes, the product of superior English engineering. Aerodynamic and lithe, he knew them both to be highly maneuverable and exceedingly spirited.

As Roland walked towards the steps he admired the medallions attached to the Jag's front grille – an RAF insignia, one for the Jaguar Club and a Union Jack. The bumper sticker around back was far less reverential… "Rugby Players Eat Their Dead."

At 72, Roland still retained vestiges of strength from a triumphant career playing rugby. Wearing dark slacks, a striped pullover and a pair of ripple-soled shoes known as "brothel creepers" by his cronies in the RAF, he was not yet daunted by age. Surprisingly athletic, he remained trim by exercising every morning and playing lots of tennis, as if determined to hold Death at bay by sheer force of will.

Roland entered the store as Howard and Marion discussed the recent troubling events and Snee rummaged through a selection of day-old pastry.

The Englishman picked up a copy of *The Bulwagga Beacon,* the local paper. "LOCH NESS INVESTIGATOR TO SEARCH FOR CHAMP," trumpeted the headlines in bold letters. Not since last winter's freight train derailment on the New York side of the lake had there been a story to rival the one he now read:

"After devoting years to the pursuit of Scotland's elusive Loch Ness Monster, a noted investigator and naturalist plans to conduct a high-tech search for 'Champ,' the renowned Lake Champlain monster."

Snee sidled up, peered over Roland's shoulder and said, "If he finds Nessie's long lost cousin, are we gonna' call it Champie?"

"Perhaps," said Roland.

"An interesting article," said Howard. "They say the investigator used an electronic gizmo that allowed him to see through the dark, peat-stained waters of Loch Ness. He took some intriguing photographs, but nothing with the monster looking you bang in the eye."

"Well then," said Marion, "he'll like our good clean lake water. You know, Howard, this is exactly what we need to get people's minds off the trouble we've been having lately – give them something positive to talk about. And just you wait, if there really is a monster swimming around in our lake, I'll bet this guy finds it."

"You are absolutely, bang-on correct," said Roland. "If a large aquatic reptile lives in the depths of Lake Champlain, I jolly well will find it."

Marion and Howard's faces lit up at the realization that they were privy to an exclusive scoop, straight from the horse's mouth, a choice bit of gossip momentous enough to help offset the damage about to be inflicted by news of the latest fatalities.

"Tell us," said Howard, "Have you actually seen the Loch Ness Monster?"

"No, not yet," Roland replied. "My findings have been tantalizing but inconclusive. The beastie remains shy and aloof. Even so, the possibility that such a creature still lives in primal isolation – a creature that should be extinct, but isn't – nags like an itch I can't quite scratch. If a reptile has indeed survived since the Cretaceous-Tertiary extinction, I very much want to be the person who finds it and documents it, once and for all."

"If there's anything I can do to help, you let me know," said Howard.

"Thank you. Actually, there is something. I wish to rent a small boat and hire a diver."

"I know just the person," said Marion, turning to the store's bulletin board. She scanned notices for a painless depilatory service, free kittens, babysitting and a handy-man. "Ah, here it is," she said, pulling out a thumbtack and handing him a business card.

SQUIRRELS IN THE ATTIC

Rock 'n Roll for every occasion
475-3417

"Their bass player is my nearest neighbor. He owns a boat and if I'm not mistaken, he's a certified scuba diver."

"Ah, good show," said Roland.

Snee paused in his eavesdropping and opened the ice-cream freezer. He selected a Ben and Jerry's Peace Pop, tore open the wrapper and took a bite.

"That'll cost you two dollars and 29 cents," said Howard.

"Highway robbery," Snee declared. "Ice cream used to be a dime." He took another bite. "Put it on my tab. Can't stay now, gotta' go and steal some scenery." A moment later he was out the door, the ice cream bar clenched in his jaws like a terrier with a rat. Howard and Marion exchanged a look of commiseration as the screen door banged shut behind him.

Roland purchased a Cadbury Fruit and Nut chocolate bar and remembered a time when they were made in England, not in Connecticut.

Chapter Eleven

Sergeant Edwards switched off the cruiser's siren and the rotating blue lights as he turned onto the Rock Cove Resort's private road. A sign admonished him to "RELAX" as he drove past the grass airstrip where the rich and powerful swooped down in Cessnas and twin-engine Beechcraft Conquistadors. He drove on, skirting the 18-hole golf course that seemed to stretch forever into the hazy distance.

Up ahead, an armada of yachts and sailboats lay moored within the diminutive lagoon that gave the resort its name. Silver-haired yachtsmen lounged in the shade of a venerable beech tree; each a retired CEO, they wore snappy tartan slacks, canary-yellow sports jackets, ascots and the radiantly white shoes favored by elderly white patriarchs.

"Ah yes," mused the sergeant. "The ruling class."

He parked his green and gold Crown Vic' alongside a fleet of immaculate black Mercedes. Having studied European history in college, the officer reflected for a moment upon the lessons imparted by the French Revolution... and the guillotine.

Nearby, couples strolled arm in arm through opulent flower gardens. Honeybees clambered amidst a profusion of gently nodding blossoms. Farther away, cozy guest cottages lined the banks of the lake. The entire resort radiated ease and gentility like a Currier and Ives print come to life – not the sort of environment the officer associated with violent death; but then, such events were always incongruous. The sergeant spoke via radio to the Mobile Crime Investigation unit. Their directions brought him across a fairway and through a patch of scrub forest. He emerged on the wrong side of a stream, but the water had fallen and he had no trouble stepping across on numerous dry rocks.

And there, surrounded by a team of forensic experts, he saw a ghastly tableau – the despoiled remains of two human beings, the ivory white of bones a shocking contrast to the crimson of lacerated muscle, sinew and cartilage. A police photographer took shots from various angles.

"Any idea what happened here?" asked Sergeant Edwards.

"No," replied the chief investigator. "I've never seen anything like this before. But if you want my opinion, these bones look as if they've been chiseled."

"Chiseled? That's the same word Hendrik, in Montpelier, used to describe the marks on the bones we removed from the Krampton Water Station. 'Gouged and chiseled,' he said. He couldn't tell me what had produced them either. Whoever did this went to an awful lot of trouble. What possible connection could there be between the bones we removed from an enclosed concrete facility and these, lying out in the open?"

"So far, there's only one commonality . . . water."

"You're right. Each incident occurred in or near the lake. But in the case of the Jet Ski death, the rider was burned beyond recognition and we can't compare bone samples."

Sergeant Edwards spent the next 20 minutes consulting with the other members of the forensic team. He learned little, other than the purpose of the weir that sat empty in mid-stream. Finally, as a throng of flies conducted their own inspections at close range, gloved personnel gathered up the remains, prior to scrutiny in the lab.

* * *

The vertical worry-line between Elsbeth J. Hawthorne's eyebrows deepened as she observed the officer's approach from her office window. In another minute her receptionist would call to say that a Sergeant Paul Edwards from the State Police waited in the lobby to see her. Elsbeth lingered for a moment on the salacious memory of their dalliance as college students, years before her marriage and subsequent control of the resort her grandfather had established a hundred years ago. It had been a torrid liaison, marked by the casual infidelity typical of many undergraduate romances. Nothing more than practice for real life, she concluded. Nevertheless, even now – all these years later – an ember still glowed deep within at the thought of him.

"Send him in," she ordered when the call came.

A moment later Sergeant Edwards stood before her, eyes shining with intelligence, shaved head shining with perspiration, muscles bulging beneath a crisply ironed uniform, service pistol bulging in its holster.

The former lovers silently appraised one another. The intervening years had not been kind to her, he realized. Strands of gray now streaked her once auburn tresses. She looked care-worn, as if weighed down by too much responsibility.

"Hello Elsbeth. It's been a while. How are you?"

She stood behind her desk and made no move to approach or shake hands.

"Very busy, Paul. Take a chair. Can I get you something cold to drink?"

"No, thank you. This is not a social call, as I'm sure you're aware. I've just returned from the crime scene. What can you tell me about the discovery of the bodies?"

"One of our grounds-keepers was out fishing when he came upon them. It must've been a shock, but he had the good sense to come to me first. I insisted we return for a second look. I was able to impress upon him the need for keeping the dreadful discovery a secret, at least till the police arrived. Fortunately, an employee found the bodies, not one of our guests. The damage to our reputation could've been considerable."

"Your reputation? Elsbeth, I'm disturbed by your apparent lack of concern for the two men butchered so close to your door."

"Of course, how insensitive of me. Who were they? And have you learned the cause of their deaths?"

"No. All I can say is that they were state wildlife officers on official business. The mobile crime lab people are on the scene as we speak. We'll know more after they've had a closer look. Off-hand, I'd say the mutilations do not appear to be consistent with those inflicted by an ax or a machete."

"Listen to me, Paul. I got a good look and I tell you, those men were eaten! Something stripped the flesh from their bones, like piranhas in South America. What else could've caused such terrible damage?"

"There are no piranhas in Vermont, Elsbeth, especially in the streams adjacent to Rock Cove's golf course."

"Of course not. Could there be a large carnivore loose out there? A catamount?"

"A possibility, although a remote one. There hasn't been a catamount sighting in ages. Tell me, have you heard of anything out of the ordinary happening on or around the lake?"

"No, not really... but come to think of it, some of our guests – VIP's – have remarked on the lack of good fishing this year. Just the other day a Supreme Court judge said he thought he'd have better luck casting a line into our swimming pool."

"I was hoping you might've heard or seen something more tangible," said Paul.

"What in the name of all that's holy could be more tangible than two half-eaten corpses, practically in my own backyard? We at Rock Cove are simply not accustomed to dealing with this sort of thing. No doubt the reporters will be here any minute, prying and sniffing around. And they, of course, will generate bad publicity – the last thing we need. With all the wet weather we've been having, business has been off, so I must ask you to conclude your investigation as quickly and quietly as circumstances will allow. May I count upon your cooperation and discretion in this matter?"

"If you're suggesting I hide the truth, Elsbeth, I'm not in a position to help."

"Now you listen to me, sergeant. I want this entire sorry mess kept under wraps. Do you understand? I cannot allow our good name to be sullied by a freak mishap, especially after last summer's salmonella outbreak. Another publicity disaster like that and the resort goes bankrupt. And if that happens, you can forget all about our long tradition of philanthropy. Do you have any idea how important we are to the vitality of this community? How many jobs we provide? Rock Cove is essential and must be protected."

The sergeant held his tongue.

"So, to clarify my position . . . The less information about this incident that leaks out, the better. Do I make myself clear?"

"Yes, Mrs. Hawthorne, perfectly clear. But let me make myself equally clear to you. My responsibility has been and will continue to be the protection of the public, regardless of the effects it may have on your reputation or your bottom line."

"I see," she said. "Perhaps you are not fully aware of the amount of influence I can bring to bear on a great number of spheres in our little corner of the world. Tomorrow, for instance, any number of local merchants would obey my directive to thwart you. You're building a new house, are you not? The delivery of the materials you require could be inexplicably delayed, or become unattainable for one reason or another. Tell me, are you aware of the amount of financial assistance we regularly provide to such worthy causes as the State Police Academy Scholarship Fund?"

"Be careful, Elsbeth. I do not take kindly to ultimatums. And this is beginning to sound a lot like blackmail."

"Bingo! You're finally getting the big picture. You never used to be so slow."

Once again, the two stared at one another, but now only the thinnest veneer of civility hid the woman's ironclad determination. She now realized that all traces of her lingering regard for the man must be ruthlessly suppressed.

The seconds ticked audibly by on the ponderous grandfather clock that stood against a wall – a presence as palpable as if the grandfather himself were there. Elsbeth broke eye contact and stood, clearly indicating an end to their meeting. "If there's nothing else, sergeant, you must excuse me. I have much to do in preparation for our upcoming Independence Day celebration."

The sergeant rose silently from his chair.

"I trust you'll keep me informed in regard to this deplorable situation," she said. Then she bestowed upon him her most insincere smile and ushered him to the door.

"Do come again, when this unfortunate business is behind us. And when you do, don't forget to bring your golf clubs… or your balls."

Chapter Twelve

Rosy-fingered clouds reached across the morning sky, as they did when Odysseus embarked upon his fateful voyage long ago. Roland and Jade sipped tea and coffee, respectively, as they sat waiting alongside the resort's basin-shaped harbor.

"What time did you agree to meet the fellow with the boat?" asked Jade as Roland scanned the broad lake with a pair of binoculars.

"I see him now," he replied. "Bang on time. I say, this place reminds me of the Lake District in England. But it must get awfully damned chilly here in the winter."

"Global warming will fix that," Jade replied.

Still hundreds of yards away, an older but still sleek blue and white Bayliner glided towards them. Behind the wheel stood a young man wearing faded denim cut-offs, sneakers and a T-shirt bearing the silk-screened image of a skull with a lightning bolt where the brain normally resides.

The cruiser drew up smoothly alongside the dock. The young man stepped off the transom and fastened a stern line to a dock-cleat. "Ahoy there," he said. "You must be Roland Humphrey. We spoke yesterday on the phone. My name is Winslow, but everyone calls me Waves."

"How do you do," said Roland. "This is Jade, my granddaughter and my assistant. Do you have any nautical superstition or problem with having a woman onboard?"

"Heck, no! She can cook and scrub for the crew!"

"Watch it, Ahab," said the young woman with green eyes and close-cropped hair as gold as a newly minted corn-flake. "I've handled catamarans that would eat your plastic stink-pot for breakfast."

"Yes, I'm sure you have," said Waves. "Come aboard and have a look around. The Moira is in good shape; the engine's recently been tuned, we've got a small refrigerator and a two-burner electric range in the galley. The shower is functional, as is the head. The previous owner lived on the seacoast, so in addition to VHF radio, there's also a LORAN navigation system – which I doubt we'll need."

"This boat is precisely what I had in mind," said Roland.

"I read the article in the local rag," said Waves. "You're here to find Champ, the Chamber of Commerce's favorite sea-monster."

"That's right," said Jade. "We're going to confirm its existence, if possible."

"Well then, you have your work cut out for you. Lake Champlain is a hundred and ten miles long. Ever been snipe hunting?"

Roland laughed and said, "Not since I was a boy, but Jade might have a go. Do I detect a hint of skepticism? You don't believe Champ exists, do you? Well, that's all right. Over the years I've become inured to the doubting Thomases of this world. Tell me this, do you believe in God?"

An odd question, thought Waves. "I believe in Godzilla. Why do you ask?"

"In my travels I've encountered three types of people: Those who believe, those who will never believe and those who would very much like to believe but cannot, at least not until they've found a compelling reason to do so. In which category are you?"

"I'll take curtain number three. But seriously, I've wasted enough time searching for God, and I found nothing beyond the simple optimism known as faith. And as far as I can tell, you either have it or you don't. Don't get me wrong; I'm not saying there isn't a god, I'm saying the truth is probably beyond our capacity to comprehend, and no amount of theologians break-dancing on the head of a pin is likely to ever change that."

"Touché," said Jade. "I too search for God. But I believe whole-heartedly – in God, in Nessie and in Champ. In my opinion, if you find one, you've found them all. And since I believe in their existence, the chances of finding them are that much better."

"Hmmm," said Waves. "I'll have to think about that."

"Let's get down to brass tacks, shall we?" said Roland. "We require unlimited access to your boat, anywhere from two weeks to a month, plus your help as an experienced scuba diver, which I'm told you are. Although I no longer dive, Jade retains her certification. Having two divers will make our task go more quickly."

"What exactly is your task?"

"I intend to deploy 24 hydrophones, exquisitely sensitive listening devices that will allow us to monitor the water in real-time."

"You're going to listen for Champ?"

"Precisely. Since this body of water is so much larger than Loch Ness, I felt the need for an entirely different approach. The loch is only 24 miles long and a mile and a half wide – a bathtub in comparison – albeit a deep one at 900 feet. Previously, my search mode was visual. This time it will be auditory."

"Well then," said Waves, "I'm your man."

"Excellent," said Roland. "I like a person who can seize an opportunity."

"There is one thing; I'm in a band and play gigs from time to time, but it shouldn't interfere. Now, as to my fee…"

Roland handed him a $500 bill and said, "Consider this a retainer."

Waves scrutinized the crisp new bill. He recognized Jackson's countenance on a twenty – it reminded him of the singer in the Moody Blues – but he could not identify the note's aristocratic face.

"Tell me when you think you deserve more," said Roland. "Now then, when can we start?"

Waves pocketed the bill and said, "We already have."

"Jolly good. The sooner we get cracking, the sooner we'll find Champ. And who knows? Maybe we'll find God as well. First, however, we must retrieve our gear."

Roland and Jade stepped onto the dock and walked to the guest cottage named "Tranquility." They soon returned, each carrying two very expensive looking aluminum suitcases.

Jade unrolled a high-resolution satellite photograph of Lake Champlain and placed it on the cockpit table. She pointed to a tiny concavity on the lake's eastern edge. "This is our position and these red dots to the north and south indicate our targets."

Roland opened one of the aluminum cases. Inside, six stainless steel cylinders lay snugly cradled, each in its own padded compartment. "The Meridian Transducer was initially designed to monitor rainfall in the distant reaches of the Pacific, but I recognized its potential as a tool in our search."

He slid open a curved panel to reveal a small Teflon valve and a light emitting diode. "We'll deploy each one at a depth of 25 feet. All you do is turn this valve clockwise till it stops. When the LED lights up, you let go and that's all there is to it. The units achieve neutral buoyancy, so they stay pretty much where we put them. Each has a transmitter with enough battery power to last six months. As I said, they are quite sensitive; capable of detecting frequencies between 10 and 22,000 Hertz."

"That's beyond the range of the human ear," said Waves. "But how will you know the difference between the sound of Champ and, say, a dog chasing a stick?"

"I've designed software to deal with that," said Jade. "Once all twenty-four transducers are in place, we record the lake's normal ambient sounds – a baseline consisting of the everyday noises made by motorboats, sailboats, swimmers, dogs chasing sticks and even fish. Once we have a catalog of their acoustic signatures, the computer filters out everything except a new signal. Once we've eliminated all extraneous input, anything that remains is worthy of our attention."

"She's awfully clever," said Roland with pride.

"Suppose you pick up an unidentified signal, what then?" asked Waves.

"Ever hear of a Nantucket sleigh-ride?"

"No, what is it?"

"In the bad old days of whale hunting," said Roland, "even before they used harpoon guns, the whalers rowed a longboat until they were close enough to their quarry to hurl a harpoon. If it struck and held, the rope played out and the whale dragged them hell for leather over the ocean. Eventually the whale grew tired and gave up the struggle, but often it took hours."

Chapter Thirteen

Dark Island acquired its name as a result of the dense, primordial forest at its core. A smothering canopy of vine-choked trees reduced the amount of daylight reaching the ground to little more than twilight. Night produced darkness so opaque that not even moonlight penetrated. When girdled in fog, the island appeared to hover. Sometimes it seemed to be sailing away, an illusion fostered by wind and a ribbon of calm water in its lee. An isolated chunk of solid ground, ignored except by seagulls, marine charts and Dr. Stanley Stryker.

Years before, after exploring its rocky inlets by canoe and the dim interior on foot, he came upon a unique geological formation at the base of the westward facing cliff; a veritable throne, carved from the living rock by the ancient conflict between ice and stone.

Stryker sat on the sun-warmed throne, admired the glories of a pollution-augmented sunset and decreed, "Here, I will build my citadel of Science."

Dark Island's previous owner was only too happy to be rid of such a useless and downright inconvenient lump of rock. Tenure at the university freed the professor from all immediate financial concerns. And over time, his invested inheritance had expanded like Smaug's glittering hoard.

Dubbed "the Fortress" by the carpenters, masons and electricians ferried across daily for months during its construction, Stryker's freshwater research laboratory gradually metamorphosed from dream, to blueprint, to reality. His mania for privacy manifest in a steadfast refusal to allow the removal of any more trees than was absolutely necessary for work to proceed.

Architectural details not often found in private dwellings were incorporated into the design. Enormous sheets of mirrored glass rose above a stone foundation to enclose the structure's first and second floors – confusing barriers responsible for the neck-breaking thud of bird hitting glass whenever a chickadee or jay mistook the reflected image for reality.

At ground level, the laboratory contained enough computers, oscilloscopes, microscopes, aquariums, beakers and test tubes to satisfy the most demanding mad scientist. (Only one thing missing, an arc of electricity rising between the V-shaped antennas of a Jacob's ladder).

The second floor contained a kitchen, living room and guest bedrooms. A rack of high-end audio gear shared the living room with a short-wave transceiver, VHS and CB radio. The structure's third floor was devoted to the master bedroom, a spacious chamber where numerous skylights afforded the professor and his wife a view of the stars at night.

Perhaps the structure's most unusual feature – a domed tower that rose to a height just below that of the tallest trees, not a minaret, but an observatory. The dome protected the largest telescope in the state of Vermont – an instrument with a 17-inch primary mirror, enough light-gathering aperture to provide spectacular views of the Milky Way's gauzy swath and to easily resolve the trapezium in the great Orion nebula.

Stryker came close to achieving energy self-sufficiency. Solar panels placed inconspicuously on the island's southwestern perimeter caught the sun's energy; batteries stored the power not consumed by appliances or the lab. Gauges displayed fluctuating voltage levels – needles dipping when clouds obscured the sun, rising again upon its reemergence. The whirling blades of two wind turbines glinted like Futurist kinetic sculpture. In an emergency, a generator provided additional electricity. Nearby, mounted on an aluminum mast disguised as a fir tree, a satellite dish and an array of telecommunications antennas received signals from near and far.

Although the professor dearly loved his communication equipment, it did little to help him communicate with his wife. Life on Dark Island remained uneventful until the day she marched into the lab, folded her arms across her chest and declared, "I've had it with this damn island. I'm leaving! You can stay here with all your toys, or you can come with me. But you can't have both. The decision is yours." She turned and walked away.

Stryker knew that an era in his life had ended. Leaving the island was simply out of the question. He'd invested too much time, effort and money. Nor had he been entirely surprised by her latest ultimatum. A year after they met, she a grad student and he a recently tenured professor, he made the mistake of acquiescing to her first ultimatum: "Either we get married, or we're through."

The ceremony had been a simple affair, tasteful and elegant. The inexorable drift apart began when she spent increasing amounts of time with friends unknown to him, people who did not include him in their social activities. And so, their lives diverged – his in pursuit of scientific Truth, hers in pursuit of gregarious fun.

Stryker knew the marriage was doomed the morning his wife disrupted breakfast with the exasperated cry, "All you ever want to talk about is literature, philosophy and science!"

The divorce had been a marvel of efficiency: Neither tearful recriminations nor wrangling over the custody of non-existent children – not even an appearance in court, just his signature on a legal document and the marriage was dead.

But now, alone on the island, he faced two options – to either hurl himself into the lake or hurl himself into his work.

Having chosen the latter, the professor often sought solace by descending to the rock throne at the base of the cliff. Most days the air smelled good and the restless water invoked meditative euphoria. But today a southwesterly wind bore the acrid reek generated by the Ticour Paper Mill.

The stink disgusted him. Disgust turned to anger at the thought of politicians seeking to not only prolong its cause, but to increase it. His anger grew as he considered the hazards threatening the lake – the rising mercury levels in game fish, PCB contamination, pesticide and agricultural runoff, plus the rapid proliferation of invasive species such as zebra mussels and the non-indigenous plants now choking the shallows.

Other, far more insidious threats loomed as well, as subtle as the increasing ultra-violet radiation reaching the Earth's surface, as pernicious as acid rain, as insidious as global warming. More than enough work to keep him busy for the next 25 years.

The professor was keenly aware of one ineluctable fact – the single most constant factor in each and every threat to the environment... Mankind. An aggressively pugnacious species, humans had become far too numerous. It was appalling. The ugly, the stupid and the infirm, all multiplying faster than flesh-eating bacteria in a Petri dish. If allowed to continue unchecked, the professor feared that humanity's rapacious appetite would eventually eradicate every last field and forest, to make way for more highways, more automobiles, more factories, more trailer parks and more shopping malls.

Stryker believed that western civilization teetered on the brink of an unprecedented economic collapse, as if the conclusion of a century-long orgy of petroleum consumption was clearly in sight, but the revelers chose instead to drown out the sound of its approach by revving up their engines.

It was one thing to drive to and from work, he knew, a necessary evil, but what of the countless overfed humans burning gasoline to blow away the leaves in their yards, burning it to trim harmless plants growing around their homes, burning it in millions of smog-belching machines in order to achieve the thrill of aimless movement without the slightest muscular exertion?

The sooner the oil ran dry, he decided, the better. Humanity could learn to do without gasoline, plastic and napalm too, for that matter. Yes, the professor concluded, the world was completely insane and its intractable stupidity was infuriating.

He was certain of one thing – drastic measures would have to be taken.

Chapter Fourteen

"Bulwagga Bay will be the center of our search radius," said Roland, jabbing the map with an index finger. "According to the locals, that's where the greatest number of Champ sightings have occurred over the years. And, where the creature spends the winter."

"Anywhere will do if you happen to be extinct," said Waves. "But eventually he'll retire and move to Florida. Let's get started."

Jade untied the stern line as Waves started the boat's Chrysler V-8. He engaged the transmission, the inboard engine rumbling louder as he pushed the throttle forward. The Moira moved away from the dock, its bow pointed west.

"Where to, Commander?"

"North. We'll deploy at the outermost positions first," said Roland.

Once beyond the cove's sheltering embrace, a southerly breeze rippled the water's surface. The chop would increase and Waves knew the outward leg would be a lot smoother than the return.

After cruising for an hour beneath a partially cloudy sky, they reached their target area and deployed the first transducer. Roland made a note in his logbook and jotted down the unit's number. The routine varied little from then on for the rest of the day: Waves and Jade took turns donning an aqualung and stepping off the transom, swaddled in black neoprene, a transducer in one hand while the other hand braced the mask.

By four in the afternoon the transducers were all in place except one. The sun's journey across the firmament had brought it well past the zenith by the time Waves placed the regulator mouthpiece between his lips and lowered his mask into position. Jade handed him the final transducer, which he held like a quarterback gripping a football.

After one final thumbs-up, he stepped off the transom and plunged into the water. The sound of the splash quickly subsided, replaced by the hiss of inhalation and exhalation. A slow upward bloom of bubbles confirmed he was no longer a clumsy terrestrial plodder held in gravity's grip, but instead, the embodiment of a sleek and sinuous Creature from the Black Lagoon.

Waves kicked his fins and descended into the algae-tinted depths. At a depth of 12 feet he paused to equalize the pressure in his ears – blowing gently through pinched nostrils to push air into the Eustachian tubes.

Translucent surface water modulated to ever-darker shades of green as he descended again, the light dwindling to an eerie twilight that was almost black. At 25 feet the water temperature had dropped to 49 degrees, visibility practically nil.

Waves opened the transducer's side panel, rotated the valve and waited for the unit to achieve neutral buoyancy. After 20 seconds the LED lit. He released the unit and the cylinder hung motionless in place. Satisfied, he began a slow ascent, careful not to rise faster than his exhaled bubbles.

He hadn't gone more than a few feet when a sudden jolting impact tore the mask away from his face. Cold, dark water blinded him and an involuntary shout of surprise nearly ejected the mouthpiece. Adrenalin pumped into his bloodstream and his heart rate raced. Groping blindly, he bumped into and then grabbed the mask. He slid it over his head, pulled it into position and purged the water by exhaling through his nose, forcing the liquid out through a tiny gap he created in the rubber seal against his forehead. The entire incident lasted less than 15 seconds.

Once again able to see what little could be seen, Waves unhooked the flashlight from his weight-belt, switched it on and probed the surrounding murk. The beam penetrated no farther than 25 feet, but there, at the edge of his peripheral vision, he detected movement. He whirled around just in time to catch a fleeting glimpse of something vanishing swiftly into the gloom.

* * *

The Moira floated at anchor amidst a forest of gently swaying masts. Roland, Jade and Waves relaxed in folding chairs, sipping Guinness and watching the sunset behind the Adirondacks. Rollicking clarinet melodies floated through the air as the Onion River Jazz Band played classic Dixieland tunes in a gazebo alongside the cove.

"Nothing like that has ever happened to me before," said Waves.

"Could it have been a muskrat?" asked Jade.

"Couldn't say. I didn't get a good look."

"Most unusual," said Roland. "Muskrats are shy creatures and they generally stay away from humans. But in any event, you're fine and all 24 units are in position."

"What's their transmission range?" asked Waves.

"Practically unlimited. They rely on the Global Positioning System."

"What happens with them once you're done?"

"Retrieval is a lot quicker than deployment," said Jade. "Each unit carries an inflatable balloon and a CO_2 cartridge. When we're ready, I'll trigger them, one by one, by remote control, once we're in the immediate vicinity. They rise to the surface and all we have to do is tool around in the boat and grab them."

Roland took another sip of Guinness and said, "It's incredible how things have changed since I first became involved in snipe hunting, as you so eloquently put it, Waves. I recall a time when a camera and patience was all that was required. Then along came bigger and better telephoto lenses, only to be replaced by side-scan sonar, although patience remains a virtue. And now, here we are, all these years later – Buck Rogers meets Jacques Cousteau."

"I once saw a photo taken at Loch Ness," said Waves. "You know the one – a long neck rising out of the water, a head somewhat like a horse's."

"Ah yes," Roland replied. "The famous shot taken by Colonel R.K. Wilson in 1936, known as 'the Surgeon's photograph' ever since. The world was a simpler place then, especially in regard to the public's gullibility. Wilson passed away a few years ago, but before he died, he held a press conference at his bedside and confessed to having carved the intriguing object in the photo from a piece of pine. Apparently, the thought of checking out with a hoax on his conscience was too much."

"Did his confession alter your belief in Nessie?" asked Waves.

"No. Oddly enough, instead of dampening my enthusiasm, it had the opposite effect. After all the sightings in the intervening years, I simply had to learn the truth. Think of all the witnesses that have come forward . . . they couldn't all have been lying, surely?"

"There was another famous photo," said Jade. "Taken right here on Lake Champlain in 1977. It made the headlines as well as Time magazine."

"Ah yes," said Roland. "The Mansi photograph."

"I missed that one," said Waves. "Tell me about it."

"It's a color shot of a long-necked creature – similar to the Surgeon's, but taken with an Instamatic from a distance of 150 feet. The print was analyzed by the Optical Sciences Center at the University of Arizona, and they concluded the water patterns surrounding the object were genuine. But unfortunately, the woman who took the shot was never able to say exactly where it was taken. Not only that, but the negative was lost."

"Sheer damn carelessness, if you ask me," said Roland.

"Not only that," said Jade. "I did some research and learned that there's a history of hoaxes perpetrated by engineering students at the University of Vermont. From time to time they'll fabricate a mechanical sea monster, a submersible contraption that looks convincing when seen from a distance."

"I'd love to see a robo-Champ," said Waves. "And I'd really like to know why there haven't been more and better photographs taken since 1977. With all the people walking around with cameras these days, you'd think by now we'd have a complete family album of Champ, Bigfoot, Sasquatch and the Jersey Devil."

Chapter Fifteen

Thick brown drapes obstructed every window in Harvey and Dot's living room, shutting out the already muted light of a cloudy afternoon. A stalled low-pressure system smothered the northeast like a monstrous gray broody hen. The television's dim glow did little to relieve the sepulchral gloom as Dot stared at the screen and Harvey dozed on the couch amidst a heap of sleeping dogs.

"Harvey! You're snoring!"

"Huh? No Dot, it was one of the dogs."

All three spaniels awoke, yawned and stretched. Max nipped at some persistent annoyance between his hind legs. Sam scratched an ear. Cricket farted.

"Okay, that's it," said Dot. "Everyone off the couch! Harvey, take the dogs outside, they've been cooped up all day."

Harvey pushed the animals away and rose to his feet, knees cracking as he limped to the glass door and slid it open. The dogs dashed through and into the yard. They nosed around for a minute, watered the bushes and then caught sight of a cyclist passing on the road beyond the fence.

Max emitted a trumpet-howl of indignation.

"Get 'em," said Harvey.

Max took off in pursuit, snarling viciously. The cyclist cursed and put on a burst of speed, unaware that the dog could not breach the barrier. Cricket emitted slathering growls, but left the exertion of an actual chase to younger paws. As the eldest of the three pets, Sam enjoyed the fewest restrictions – much the way an aged convict achieves the status of a trustee. The dog ignored the rider, trotted past the barn and down the winding path towards the metal stairs and the water's edge.

Sam liked to bark at the water. The dog stood in the shallows and gave the lake a thorough barking, then lapped up a snoot-full of water. After a final bark, he climbed the steps, trotted along the path, across the lawn and towards the house, where Harvey and the other two dogs stood waiting by the door. Sam entered the house, his wet paws embossing the hardwood floor.

Harvey had just settled onto the couch when Dot pointed the TV remote at him and said, "If you leave that dog out there alone one more time, I'll play hackie-sack with your scrotum!"

"What's the problem, Dot? The dog's gotta' take a dump."

"You shouldn't let him roam at will. There are rabid raccoons out there and skunks and eagles and god only knows what else."

"All right, already," said Harvey, hoping to forestall any further nagging.

At that moment Sam made a strange gagging sound. Harvey and Dot looked on as the dog produced a sound eerily similar to Dot's voice – not a bark, but a peculiar guttural noise on the threshold of a bark.

"Haaar... haaarrph... haaarrrphy!"

They watched as the dog repeated the feat.

"Haaaarrrgh, haaarrrphy!"

Once again, like a parrot, the dog duplicated Dot's own bark. Then he lowered his head, opened his jaws wide and out poured a foul-smelling liquid, replete with chunks of half-digested chow. The spaniel collapsed onto the hearthrug, paws quivering, and lay still.

"Harvey! Don't just sit there, do something!"

Harvey kneeled alongside the inert pet and looked closely.

"Sam's dead."

"Get outa' here!" said Dot as she lurched from the recliner to see for herself. "He can't be dead! He was fine, till you let him out."

"No, he was an old dog and now he's gone. Thirteen years is a long life for a spaniel. Don't forget, he was arthritic and practically deaf."

Dot returned to her chair, struggling to hold back tears. "That damned dog never did listen to me, only did what he wanted to. Harvey! Where's Cricket? Where's Max?"

"Relax. Cricket is right there on the couch. Max is asleep in the bedroom. There's only one thing we can do for Sam now and that's bury him."

Harvey rolled the dog's body in the oval rug and then he carried the bundle outside and placed it in the wheelbarrow used to haul firewood. Cricket looked on. After grabbing a shovel from the barn, Harvey pushed the wheelbarrow down the path and into the cool, moist woods. He turned aside from the path and dug a hole large enough to contain the body and deep enough to dissuade some other creature from digging it up.

Harvey placed the dog in the grave, rug and all, and then shoveled the loose soil back in, tamping it down with the back of the shovel. After covering the mound with a layer of heavy stones, Harvey stood and wondered if a prayer might be appropriate.

"Okay Sam," he said. "You always were a stupid mutt."

Chapter Sixteen

The Ticour Paper Mill squatted on the edge of the lake like a Gothic nightmare from the Industrial Revolution. The immense steel structure trembled and groaned as it gorged on the timber felled by chainsaws called "man-killers" by the men who wielded them. Old-growth trees toppled and crashed; skidders hauled the logs from the deep woods to flatbed trucks for transport to the mill. There, hydraulic claws grabbed and tumbled the trunks into an insatiable maw – to be shredded and liquefied – prior to conversion into toilet paper and tabloid newsprint. Like the devil's favorite fumerol, smoke belched continuously from a single, towering brick chimney, the acrid vapors pluming and billowing into the vast waste receptacle known as the sky.

After surviving another week amidst the noise and fury of machinery that could easily chew up a man and spit out bloody chunks, Hank and Zeke trudged wearily across the employee parking lot. Too tired to speak, they clutched empty lunchboxes in calloused hands well acquainted with the guts of fish, the necks of chickens and the by-products of cows. The two men climbed into Hank's old Ford Galaxy. They leaned back and closed their eyes for a minute's worth of silent recuperation.

Born and raised in Krampton, Hank and Zeke became best friends in elementary school, where they endured the interminable boredom inflicted by teachers that focused their attention upon the brighter students. Then, it was on to junior high, where the secret of doing math with letters from the alphabet (instead of numbers) remained stubbornly elusive. At the age of 14, Hank and Zeke shared their first illicit six-pack of Budweiser and soon thereafter a pack of Trojans – and, coincidentally, the affections of a flighty and neurotic brunette named Jeanne.

Hank and Zeke both dropped out of high school in their sophomore year.

They spent a lazy summer fishing and drinking beer before joining the moiling ranks of wage-slaves at the mill. They were good workers and the resulting paychecks assured them a steady diet of potato chips, Pepsi and pizza, to say nothing of lottery tickets, cigarettes and beer.

* * *

Hank opened his eyes and started the Galaxy. A moment later the car accelerated into the gathering darkness: Destination – Beebe's Thirst Parlor.

An archaic brick edifice soon emerged from the gloaming like some cruel orphanage in a novel by Dickens. The site of a saloon by one name or another for the last hundred years, the Thirst Parlor offered little to identify itself, just the buzzing neon sign in the window that said "BEER."

Hank and Zeke entered as the jukebox blasted "Born To Be Wild" for the ten-thousandth time. Gyrating couples crowded the dance floor as the mill-hands took their customary places on stools at the bar. The bartender eyed them as she lit a cigarette and blew twin gusts of exhaust through her nostrils, reinforcing the indelible odor of stale beer, stale nicotine and stale urine. She uncapped and slid two cold bottles across the bar. Hank grabbed one and took a long pull – the kind of soul-quenching guzzle that separates the sippers of white wine from the real men.

"You know, Zeke, the Fishing Derby's gonna' start a week from tomorrow and I been thinkin' about it. I'm convinced there's a way we can win that cruiser."

"Course there is," said Zeke. "All we gotta' do is catch the mother of all fish."

Hank drained his bottle, smacked his lips and signaled for another round.

"Every summer one of them rich, porky flatlanders drives up in a goddamn Winnebago, catches a humongous fish and wins the grand prize. They do it every year, I tell 'ya, always someone from Connecticut or Pennsylvania, and it just ain't fair."

Zeke munched a handful of stale, rubbery popcorn as Hank spun his stool to face the cue-stick-toting figures standing in the dim penumbra cast by a lamp suspended above the pool table. After completing a 360-degree rotation, he said, "Listen up, Zeke, I've got one hell of an idea."

"Okay, Hank, I'll bite, what's on your mind?"

Hank glanced around and then spoke in a low, conspiratorial tone.

"What if the two of us got hold of some monster fish, see. We get a big one from my cousin up north – he's always pulling 'em out of Lake Willoughby. We bring it back alive in a barrel full a' water. Then, once the Derby starts, we smuggle it out onto the lake before dawn, fix a hook into it and let it go. Later, we reel it in like we just caught it. Then, we go to the weigh-in station. You and me win the grand prize and no one's the wiser!"

Hank paused as the enormity of the proposed fraud sank in. Both men had a clear notion of the penalty if caught: Public disgrace, a hefty fine and an all-expense-paid vacation, courtesy of the Vermont Corrections Department.

Zeke swallowed more beer as he considered the risk. Then his face split into a crooked grin and he said, "That's one bitch of an idea, Hank. And best of all, it don't hurt no one. Not like a real crime at all. Shit . . . I say we go for it! You call your cousin first thing tomorrow. Tell him he's got a week to get out there and catch us something huge, a monster that'll knock everyone's eyes out."

"Two more long-necks," ordered Hank.

The conspirators clinked their bottles and toasted one another's health and cunning.

"Yes sir, I'm gonna' take a vacation for the rest of my life," chuckled Zeke.

Nearby, a pool player racked and then broke with a loud CLACK! The billiard balls spun from one end of the cigarette-scorched green felt to the other, caromed off the sides at various angles and

came to rest – all except the 8-ball, which rolled into a corner pocket and disappeared.

Chapter Seventeen

The water jetting from the fountain sparkled as Sergeant Edwards walked across the leafy green heart of the UVM campus. Although the university continued to expand – erecting ever more grandiose buildings – the quad looked much the same as when he'd hurried to class as an undergraduate. The trees had grown taller, the students younger; backpacks remained the preferred means of textbook conveyance and Frisbees still vied for air superiority. Nowadays, he suspected, the squirrels living in the trees all had advanced degrees in Forestry.

Memories of Elsbeth and their stormy relationship crossed the sergeant's mind as he scrutinized the four-story Gothic structure looming before him. Festooned with spires, cornices and copulas, a coterie of weather-stained gargoyles squatted high above on parapets – faces leering, mouths open, tongues dangling.

The officer walked on and approached a throng of budding young intellectuals in paint-spattered black. Art students, he realized; smoking Camels and no doubt convinced they were redefining the boundaries of coolness. Edwards continued on and drew near the Science department – a featureless mauve building that resembled corporate headquarters for an insurance company.

After consulting the directory on the lobby wall, Edwards rode the elevator to the top floor, walked a lengthy corridor and knocked on the door to Professor Stryker's office.

"Go away," an irate voice responded from within. "Office hours are between two and four on Tuesdays and Thursdays."

"State Police, open up."

The professor squelched his annoyance, opened the door and said, "Sergeant Edwards, we meet again. What brings you to the ivy-choked tower of Academia?"

"Hello professor. I'm doing some follow-up on the Jet Ski fatality. We've just learned the identity of the young man who was killed at your island. His vehicle was parked near the boat landing and it was a simple matter to trace the registration to the owner. The late Richard Tobias was enrolled here at the university, which has little bearing on the case, except for one thing: He was one of your students. The odds for such a coincidence are intriguing, to say the least."

"Indeed, the death of Mr. Tobias spoiled a perfect afternoon."

"Yours or his? Never mind; I'm hoping you can shed some additional light on the incident."

"Yes, he was one of my tadpoles. But as I've already explained, I heard the sound of the crash and called the authorities. That's all I can tell you."

"Mr. Tobias holds the dubious distinction of being the first person to die on Lake Champlain while riding a personal watercraft," said the sergeant.

"He may have been the first but he won't be the last."

"You don't say."

"I do say. Sprained wrists and neck injuries from those infernal machines are common – only an idiot would own one – but statistically, it stands to reason, the more they proliferate, the more accidents will occur."

"Tell me professor, was he a good student?"

"No, Mr. Tobias had yet to distinguish himself in the academic arena."

"Any idea why he would drive a Jet-Ski into a sheer rock wall?"

"How should I know? Maybe he was talking on a cell-phone and lost control. What do you think?"

"I'd say he either did it on purpose – a suicide, which is unlikely – or else he was trying to get away from something or someone, but that's just my gut instinct."

"Instinct is a powerful force, to be sure," said the professor. "But as a scientist, I do not care to speculate. I do, however, look forward to a time when all such internal combustion-dependent recreational vehicles are banned – every last ATV, snow-mobile and go-kart."

Curious to see how far Stryker would go in his diatribe against the trappings of a modern technological society, the sergeant said nothing.

"Officer, have you ever considered just how enslaved we've become by the almighty piston? Once, it served us, but no more. We serve it. Oil is now more essential than mother's milk. As a result, we've become a lazy, corpulent species that sits on its fat buttocks and drives lawn tractors instead of pushing mowers with blades that spin via muscle power. I tell you, internal combustion threatens all life on our planet."

"What is it about gas engines that upsets you the most?" asked Sergeant Edwards.

"Although I despise both pollution and laziness, it's the noise I find most infuriating. Go outside and what do you hear? The incessant roar of engines! Go all the way to the Arctic or deep into the Amazon and you'll not escape the noise. An idiot chorus of motorcycles, chainsaws and aircraft inundates us day and night, the howl of weed-whackers and leaf-blowers rising above it all!"

"Some might call that the price of progress."

"Progress! The only progress we're making is towards mass extinction. Did you know that between 40 and 70 different species become extinct every day, and all because of us? It's staggering! Science has yet to even name much of Earth's biodiversity, but the decimation continues unchecked."

"Those are sobering facts," the sergeant admitted, looking at his wristwatch. "I have only two more questions. With over a hundred miles of lake to chose from, why did Richard Tobias choose your island?"

"Just lucky," the professor replied with a wry smile. "And the last question?"

"Where is your wife?"

The question caught Stryker off guard, but only momentarily.

"The woman divorced me and I've not heard from her since. She intended to travel and could be anywhere by now – Mongolia, Tibet, god only knows."

The professor gestured towards a 30-gallon aquarium filled with green liquid.

"Before you go, officer, have a look at my indoor swamp. Countless microorganisms flourish here under my enlightened auspices, a self-sufficient ecosystem teeming with protozoa, copepods, daphnia, rotifers and hydra. Look there, on the bottom, the cadis-fly larva are building protective enclosures, but it won't do them any good. Soon there'll be dragonfly larva so aggressively hostile as to make Ripley's alien look benign in comparison."

"And the point to all this?" asked the sergeant.

"Predation, the foundation of life! Consider my little bowl of primordial soup a metaphor for our planet. As long as I add fresh lake water from time to time to counteract evaporation, my jittering dots of protoplasm will continue to devour one another, just like every other creature on this pullulating pill we call Earth."

"What of the vegetarians, the herbivores?"

"They exist for one purpose only, to feed the carnivores. There is, however, one glaring exception . . . Humanity. As consummate predators we enjoy our position atop the food chain. Other than sharks and the occasional rogue grizzly, there's not much in the wild to threaten us. And so, we've become a voracious monoculture that has learned little other than how to maneuver efficiently from one hamburger emporium to the next."

"You forget one thing in your cosmology," said Sergeant Edwards. "Since nature no longer provides us with predatory threats, we've assumed that responsibility ourselves. Humanity is now most threatened by other humans."

"Indeed," replied the professor. "Quite perceptive for a policeman. I salute you."

Chapter Eighteen

Dot noticed at the tapered brown object lying on the bottom of the toilet bowl and hollered, "Harvey! For the love of god, flush the goddamn toilet after you use it!"

Harvey looked up from the latest issue of Penthouse and said, "Huh? What are you talking about? I always flush. I am, in fact, completely housebroken."

"Oh yeah? Well, get a load of this. There's a turd in the bowl."

Harvey hoisted himself off the couch and walked across the living room to the nearer of the two bathrooms. He peered into the empty bowl. "I don't see anything."

Dot looked down and scowled. "It was there a moment ago."

"Get real," Harvey grumbled, returning to the couch, now occupied by Cricket and Max. "Off!" he commanded. They complied, albeit reluctantly.

After pushing the handle and watching the water whirl and flush, Dot slid her sweatpants to the floor and was about to lower her rump onto the seat when she noticed the brown object peeking out of the drain hole once more.

"Harvey! It's back," she shouted, pulling up her pants.

"Keep your hair on, I'm coming."

The dogs sidled back onto the couch.

"There," she said, looking him in the eye and pointing triumphantly at the fixture.

Harvey looked again into an empty bowl.

"I tell you, I saw it right there," Dot whined.

"Dot, I think maybe we should talk to the doctor about adjusting your medication."

"Don't give me that, I know what I saw. And besides, I need to use the bathroom, so get out!"

Harvey shrugged and retreated an instant before Dot slammed the door. Cricket and Max watched his approach with palpably guilty consciences.

"Off!" he commanded.

Exasperated, Dot flushed the toilet and checked to make sure it had done the trick. Thus assured, she dropped her pants and sat.

The mysterious object reappeared.

A lamprey.

The creature peered through beady black eyes, then slithered up the side of the bowl and pressed its circular oral hood onto the woman's flaccid left cheek. She felt its cold wet kiss but did not react until several tiny teeth punctured her skin.

"HARVEY!" she shrieked, leaping to her feet. "Something bit me!"

The lamprey plopped into the water and wriggled back up the drain-hole.

The henpecked husband jumped up and the dogs howled. He rushed in to reexamine the porcelain bowl. "Whadda'ya' mean, something bit you? Dot, there's nothing there." He flushed it again and used a plumber's helper to force the water down and away in one long guttering swallow.

"Harvey, look at my ass and tell me if I'm bleeding."

"Turn around and hold still. There's a drop of blood, just a prick. You must've gotten a splinter from that old wooden seat. Go and use the other bathroom."

"I will, but first, I want my Walther. Go and get it, now!"

Knowing better than to argue, Harvey left Dot standing with cane held aloft, ready to wallop anything that came near. He returned and handed her a zippered black leather bag. "Here, but be careful. I'm going out to do some work on the pool."

If Dot was Harvey's burden, the pool was his sanctuary. Situated a short distance behind the house, the lap-pool measured 60 feet long, 20 feet wide and had a uniform depth of four feet. Although he'd been fired as coach of the swim-team at the prestigious Horace Mann school in New York City, Harvey was not about to relinquish the poolside rituals that had sustained him, nor the fond memories of young women endowed with powerful shoulders, narrow waists and perfect derrieres swathed in sheer black nylon.

Harvey's palms were still tender from the zebra-mussel wounds, so he donned a pair of work gloves, tossed a couple of chlorine sticks into the pool and then opened a valve hidden beneath a metal plate. Within seconds fresh lake water began to gush from an aperture located halfway down the pool's wall, thereby raising the water level at an imperceptible rate.

A number of frogs leapt into the water as he approached with a net attached to a long aluminum pole. He scooped one up and catapulted it into the woods in what would be its longest jump ever; then he began to harvest the dead leaves floating at the surface.

An unpleasant surprise awaited him – a dead raccoon – afloat in a nasty bouillabaisse. The animal had fallen into the water the night before, only to claw frantically at the cement wall until it could no longer hold its head above the water. The dripping corpse was heavy and bent the pole as Harvey hoisted it up and out of the pool. He transferred the remains to a shovel and carried it some distance into the woods before dumping it where the flies, ants and bacteria could get to work on it.

Harvey spent the next two hours raking up fallen branches and twigs prior to mowing the lawn. Only then did the plastic flamingos, the chaise lounges and the bug-zapper emerge from the barn to take up their positions around the blue oasis.

By then the water level had risen to normal so Harvey closed the intake valve. But without its protective nozzle, the hose sucked in lake water and a dozen lampreys.

Lengthening shadows bisected the grass around the pool with stripes of emerald and dark green. Mosquitoes vectored in, intent upon Harvey's blood, but he was too hot to care. Nor did he mind the mat of brown leaves still carpeting the bottom of the pool. The former couch removed his glasses, stripped off his jeans and sweaty T-shirt like a snake shedding its skin. He stood with knees bent, toes curled over the rim of the pool and said, "On your mark... get set..."

At the "bang" of an imaginary starting pistol, he lunged forward in a racing dive, landing flat, pulling with fluid strokes and kicking hard. He swam to the far wall, turning his head to snatch a breath every few strokes, and then executed another kick-turn. Halfway across he felt a soft collision against his side, and then others on his shoulders and back.

Still plenty of frogs to be evicted, he thought.

After a third lap Harvey grasped the stainless steel ladder, climbed three steps and stood on the sun-warmed concrete. A moment later he glanced down and saw the lampreys clinging to his torso.

"Sumbitchin' whore-mother," he gasped as he tore them off, one after another. The lampreys had not yet bitten. Suction alone held them on. The displaced creatures squirmed at his feet, wriggled over the edge and fell back into the water. He grabbed the last one, or so he thought, unaware of the lamprey still clinging to his lower back.

Needle-sharp teeth punctured his flesh.

Harvey twisted and spun as pain receptors suddenly blared. Warm blood filled the lamprey's oral hood. Corrosive enzymes bathed the wound as repeated thrusts of a blade-tipped tongue cut deeper into Harvey's living tissue. He stumbled and fell. The rim of the pool raked an abrasion from thigh to armpit as he skidded into the water.

Eleven angry lampreys attacked.

Harvey gripped the ladder to haul himself out a second time, up one step and then a second, but his arms and legs grew heavy and he collapsed – half in and half out – paralyzed, as helpless as a flounder on a cutting board.

The lampreys adhering to his thighs and calves lashed their tails and pulled him back into the water. He sank to the bottom, wide-eyed and conscious.

And in those moments of unprecedented torment, shortly before the void claimed him, Harvey broke one of the cardinal rules that govern all pools – a law he had not violated since he was six years old. Through the red haze of agony and the horror at being eaten alive in his own cherished pool, he recalled his father's stern admonition… "Never piss in the pool."

Chapter Nineteen

Hot breezes spanked the warm Silurian sea as the plesiosaur idled at the surface, sculling gently with paddle-shaped fins. Large eyes peered from above a narrow jaw lined with a double row of stiletto teeth, a small but serviceable weapon for biting and tearing. The plesiosaur lowered its head as a pteranodon swooped low, skimming the surface for fish, buoyed on thermal currents and a 16-foot wingspan.

The plesiosaur watched and waited . . . then struck.

With a lunge and a snap of its jaws, it snagged a wing, tore through the membrane and crushed hollow bones. No longer a graceful denizen of the air, the pteranodon crumpled. The plesiosaur dragged it under and tore out the flight muscles, devouring the most nourishing parts first.

The attack had not gone unnoticed.

A tylosaurus loomed in the depths, propelled by lateral sweeps of an immense crocodilian tail and four powerful flippers. Too late, the plesiosaur sensed danger. A moment later a larger array of cutlery scissored shut on its long, graceful neck, killing it instantly. The attacker seized its victim's underbelly and spun, wrenching away huge chunks of meat. A blood-cloud expanded as schools of little yellow and blue belemites darted in and out, snapping up tiny bits.

A lapse of vigilance turned the hunter into the hunted.

A kronosaurus ascended at great speed, its mouth packed with serrated teeth the size of bayonets. Doom drew ever nearer until the cavernous maw blotted out any chance of escape. The jaws thundered shut... an instant later, Stanley Stryker lurched awake – disoriented, bathed in sweat, pinioned by a twisted sheet.

The nightmare faded, but not the conviction that he had become an entree on nature's rapacious menu. Although dawn had yet to smudge the sky, there would be no more sleep, and so, the professor arose and staggered from his bed.

* * *

The lab's overhead fluorescent tubes cast a harsh glare as Stryker set to work pouring ingredients into a machine that mixed, compressed and then spat hundreds of marble-sized pellets into a hopper. He filled a pail with the pellets and carried it outside into thick predawn fog. Sickly yellow light from a waning half moon illuminated the ghostly vapor as he descended along a path to the rocks bordering the island's western flank.

At the water's edge he stepped onto the exposed crowns of submerged boulders, striding from one noggin of rock to the next until he stood atop an isolated pulpit some 30 feet from shore. There, swathed in ethereal mist, he was reminded of the horror movies he had loved as a child – not only the haunted castles perched above daunting cliffs, or the crawling eye that moved within a frigid cloud, but the many creatures that ran amok after absorbing too much radiation; the tarantula larger than a house, or the colony of colossal ants – an implacable bestiary bent upon the destruction of Mankind – all created and ultimately vanquished by Science.

Stryker smiled as he reached into the pail and began to broadcast handfuls of pellets in a wide arc. The offering flew into the fog and hit the water with a plopping sound. He set the empty pail at his feet and waited. A minute or two later the hidden surface began to churn and boil. And as the agitation increased the professor held his arms out as if to deliver a benediction.

The mysterious commotion subsided abruptly. Only then did he lower his arms, retrieve the pail and return along the steppingstones to the shore.

Chapter Twenty

Other people were out in the thick, choking fog on this, the opening day of the Fishing Derby. The darkest hour before dawn found Hank pushing a wheelbarrow the length of a rickety wooden dock towards a rowboat, where Zeke sat smoking a cigarette, waiting. The wheelbarrow held a large plastic barrel, which in turn held many gallons of water and a magnificent trout of a size not seen around Lake Champlain in years.

Maneuvering the barrel into the rowboat was difficult; both men grunted with the exertion, sloshing and spilling much water in the process. Once aboard and centered for balance, Zeke used a bucket to scoop up and replenish the spilled water. The trout, their unwitting accomplice, lay inert, gills barely moving, its length curved to conform to the shape of its blue plastic prison.

"Couldn't ask for better weather," said Hank. "This pea-soup'll hide us perfectly. By the time the sun burns it off, you and me'll be this year's big derby winners."

"What do we do with the barrel after we dump 'em out?" asked Zeke, "We sure as shit can't show up at the weigh-in with it."

"Simple. After we hook the fish and let him go, we dump the barrel over the side. I'll fill it and let it sink. I'm hoping the fresh water will perk our guy up. He don't look too happy."

"That's using the 'ol noodle," said Zeke. "Can't be too careful."

"Do we have the sandwiches and beer? Good. We're gonna' be out long enough to do some serious fishing. Can't show up with the winning fish ten minutes after the contest begins – it would look mighty suspicious. We should put out our other lines too, maybe catch us a bonus."

Hank sat at the bow while Zeke began to row away from shore. Only the creaking of the oarlocks and the distant cry of a loon punctuated the stillness as the fog enveloped them. Still faintly visible, the half moon paled as the eastern sky gradually changed from charcoal gray to deepest ultramarine.

"We'll wait a little before we use the motor," advised Hank. "Nobody can see us, but I'm not takin' any chances."

Zeke rowed with a steady cadence until Hank said, "That's enough, start 'er up. It's time we found the perfect spot to catch us a real monster."

The old Evinrude caught on the second pull and belched oil smoke; a small blue cloud that hung intact in the motionless air. Zeke twisted the throttle and the motor chugged like an eggbeater, propelling them further into the broad lake.

"Where do you figure we should go, Hank? And how long should we wait?"

"I say we relax and enjoy the morning. We'll know when the time's right."

"Do you remember when Abe's wife caught a humongous trout and kept it in her bathtub for a week? The crazy old lady moved it outside to a fresh-water spring; even had a cord through a gill so it couldn't swim away. I don't know what she fed it, but every time I came around she'd say, 'Would you like to see my trout?' We'd walk to the spring and she'd pull up this huge fish. It lived for years!"

"What about that 36-inch northern pike I caught," said Hank. "I thought I'd hooked a buoy! Hand me a beer, will 'ya. Fish stories always make me thirsty. One thing's for sure – I'll be jiggered if anyone catches anything half as big as ours. Hell, you know how miserable the fishin's been lately; you're lucky if you catch a cold."

After twenty minutes they reached the middle of the lake. Hank decided they'd gone far enough. "Kill the motor, Zeke. We'll let our guy go so he can freshen up. But first, a toast: Here's to ya' Mr. Trout!" Hank raised his beer in salute, chugged most of it and then poured the last drops into the barrel before tossing the empty can over the side.

"Last call for alcohol," said Zeke, flinging his empty can over a shoulder.

"Okay, wedge 'em with an oar, while I grab him and set the hook." Once the hook was firmly implanted in the fish's jaw, Hank lifted it out of the barrel and lowered it into the lake. The stunned creature lingered at the surface for a moment, drawing water past its gills, then swiped its tail and vanished into the depths.

"Catch 'ya later," said Zeke.

The men tipped the barrel to drain the water, then pushed it over the side. Hank held it under until it was full before letting go. Zeke cracked open two more beers and handed one to his buddy.

As daylight grew it transformed the two fishermen from a uniform gray to their normal colors. The air temperature rose and the fog slowly lifted as Earth's nearest star flooded the sky with radiance. When at last it cleared the mountains, Sol's rays gilded everything it touched – the rowboat, the dozen or so other boats scattered about the lake and the eastern flanks of the Adirondacks.

* * *

Untouched by light, a lamprey rested on the lake's silted bottom, deep in the opaque, empty void. After seven years of living in a stream as a stationary filter feeder, it was no longer a harmless larva, but instead, an aggressive, sexually mature predator embarking upon life in open water.

The lamprey had achieved a length of 17 inches.

It's heart rate was slow, its respiration relaxed. It did not inhale, but instead contracted its bronchial basket to expel water through gill pouches. Then, like a sponge that has been squeezed and released, the subsequent expansion drew fresh water over its gill tissues.

Although the lamprey had poor eyesight, 250 million years of evolution had endowed it with a sensory organ appropriate to its needs. Below the bronchial pores on its head lay an area capable of producing an electrical field – not the 500 volts generated by its South American cousins, but an exquisitely sensitive target-acquisition system. With it, the lamprey probed for traces of amines in the water – the smell of fish – six tiny papillae tuned to the frequency of flesh.

A rock bass swam into the parasite's sensory field.

A curtain of silt rose as the lamprey slithered forward, swerving from side to side in a series of S-shaped undulations. When only ten centimeters separated them, the lamprey's mouth slit expanded into a wide circular orifice studded with concentric rings of spiky orange teeth. Suddenly it darted forward and fastened its oral hood to the fish's body, via suction. Alarmed but unhurt, the bass fought by slewing and twisting erratically, but the harder it struggled, the tighter the lamprey's grip.

The fish soon grew tired and ceased its efforts, the signal for the lamprey to rip away the scales with its teeth. But instead of tearing out pieces of flesh, as some species do, the lamprey enlarged the hole – jabbing with a blade-tipped tongue – prior to flooding the wound with digestive enzymes to dissolve the tissue into an easy-to-swallow paste.

To this end, Mother Nature had resorted to her recipe book of venom to concoct a potent variation on an old theme – a knockout punch, aided by mutation – containing highly corrosive digestive fluids, a walloping dose of endorphins, a dash of alkaloids and a soupcon of nerve toxin thrown in for good measure. Once the enzymes entered the fish's bloodstream, total paralysis ensued. The fish died – literally doped to the gills – yes, but it died a happy fish.

* * *

Two hours and two six-packs later, Hank and Zeke drifted on an indolent beery tide beneath a sun now halfway between the horizon and the zenith.

"What 'a 'ya say Zeke, old sports-fan, the fish aren't biting, as usual; we've been out here long enough. I say we haul in the big catch of the day."

Zeke picked up the rod with the line connecting them to their dreams and began to reel in the monofilament. "Our guy is still hooked. I can feel the weight."

"That's good. Bring him in slow, we don't wanna' screw up now. As soon as he's up close to the surface I'll get the net under him."

With one quick motion Hank scooped up the fish and dumped it, net and all, onto the bottom of the rowboat. The sopping bundle flopped once, twice and lay still.

"Okay," said Hank. "Open the net and let's take a gander at our lucky winner."

"I'll drink to that," said Zeke, swallowing the last of a warm beer and pitching the empty can into the lake. The bundle at his feet flapped energetically as he reached down to unravel the netting. "Whoa there, big fella. You ain't goin' nowhere."

Zeke untangled the net and both men stared in disbelief.

Lampreys clung to their prize trout.

"Quick, get 'em off," ordered Hank.

Zeke grabbed one in each hand, but the slippery creatures slid through his grasp and began to coil their sinuous lengths. When he reached down to try again, something unexpected happened – two lampreys released their hold, turned with surprising speed and thrust forward to entwine his forearms.

"What the…?" he muttered, flinging his arms out and standing abruptly. The rowboat rocked and nearly tipped as he struggled to dislodge them.

Hank watched as the lampreys sank their teeth into Zeke's biceps; a moment later Zeke went limp and tumbled over the side with hardly a splash. Hank stared, transfixed with horror, as his buddy's inert body sank, receding ever so slowly into the chilly green depths, Zeke's eyes fixed imploringly on his own.

The remaining lampreys abandoned the fish and squirmed across the rowboat's wet bottom, forcing Hank to back away. There was nowhere to go except to stand on the stern-seat as the repulsive yet strangely fascinating onslaught drew closer. When only two feet separated predators from prey, the lampreys began thrashing their tails.

Hank wracked his brain for an idea, but it was hopeless: The oars lay out of reach and there was nothing he could use as a weapon. He searched in vain for a boat within hailing distance, but the nearest was at least a mile away.

Now only a couple of feet away, the lampreys wriggled up both sides of the rowboat, then across the horizontal seat to within inches of Hank's bare feet. He wished he'd left his shoes on as he stomped the one closest with his heel, smashing it into a bloody gob. Undeterred, the lampreys moved closer. Hank tried to kick them away, but there were too many. As the distance shrank they lunged at his feet, forcing him to hop from one foot to the other. Finally, he played his last desperate card and dove over the side into the water.

The splash quickly subsided.

Ripples expanded and dissipated.

The surface became a smoothly undulating veneer once more.

* * *

An hour later another fisherman spotted the empty rowboat and reported it to the State Police via cell-phone. Eventually the police arrived aboard a swift, twin-engine craft, but all they found in the rowboat were several fishing rods with lines still out, the mutilated remains of a large fish with a hook set in its jaw and a small convoy of empty beer cans afloat nearby.

The enigma grew more baffling when the police discovered a blue plastic barrel suspended in the water nearby, just below the surface. A trooper drained it and pulled it out. The police boat towed the abandoned rowboat to shore and deposited it at the Krampton boat ramp, where two Fishing Derby officials sat at a folding table, with a scale, patiently awaiting the arrival of lucky anglers with their catch.

Chapter Twenty-One

Not everyone in Krampton arose before the sun. Waves had played a gig with Squirrels in the Attic the night before and didn't get home till after three in the morning. The telephone's first ring at eight jangled his subconscious. The second woke him. By the seventh ring he knew the caller was not about to give up, but it wasn't till the tenth that he lifted the receiver and mumbled, "Hello."

"Ah, there you are at last," said Roland. "We need to get cracking immediately. We've been monitoring the transducers and the latest readings are unprecedented. This could be what we've been waiting for! Meet us at Rock Cove as quickly as possible."

Waves squinted at the clock and said, "I'll be there in approximately half an hour."

Forty-five minutes later, after feeding his goldfish – Rumble, Wow and Flutter – and then wolfing down a bowl of Cheerios, a bagel and a cup of coffee, Waves steered the Moira into the cove and alongside the dock, where Roland and Jade sat waiting. They climbed aboard and Waves said, "So, what's up? Have you made contact with the unknown?"

"We've certainly made contact with something," said Jade. "Here, put these on."

Waves donned padded headphones and all airborne sounds were subsumed by a subtle hiss made all the more puzzling by subtle but rhythmic fluctuations.

"What am I hearing?" he asked.

"I have no idea, but I'm pretty sure it isn't man-made. Watch what happens when I switch from auditory to much higher wavelengths." Jade tapped a few keys on the laptop; the computer screen displayed overlapping patterns that resembled oscilloscopic waveforms.

"This is the computer's translation of electrical energy into a visual analog," she said.

"Electrical energy?"

"Micro-voltages, to be precise," said Roland. "Not the same as the alternating current you and I are accustomed to. These are much weaker – more akin to nerve impulses than anything else – but the sheer magnitude is quite extraordinary."

Additional keystrokes resulted in a satellite's eye view of New England, seen from a geo-synchronous orbit 23,000 miles out in space. The lake's 110-mile length was not even visible until Jade zoomed in and centered the image.

"Those green blotches represent the areas of greatest signal strength," said Jade. "Something's creating one hell of an electrical field and I'd like to know what."

"Why so many?" asked Waves. "If it's Champ, shouldn't there be only one?"

"Yes, but even so, this could be nothing more than signal break-up or some form of electronic reflection – a bug in the system, gremlins – damned if I know."

Jade adjusted the contrast to enhance the image and zoomed in closer, watching as the blotches slowly changed their position. "They appear to be converging on that little island."

"So they are," said Roland. "If whatever's producing these signals is headed towards that island, then we had better do so as well."

Waves pointed the Moira's bow west and gunned the engine. The boat picked up speed, traversed the cove and within minutes they were in mid-lake, headed south, surrounded by a vaporous lavender envelope – a vast empty expanse in which sky and lake merged seamlessly. Numerous fishing boats were visible, scattered in the distance.

All three sat quietly, deep in the introspection fostered by close proximity to a trillion gallons of water: Roland savored the aroma of algae as he watched the wake carved by the Moira – an expanding swathe demarcating their passage. Roland pondered the arc of his life and wondered if his course through time left a wake of its own.

Jade contemplated the challenge of unthwarting her as-yet-thwarted ambition: To distinguish herself in a world teeming with others in her field, all equally hell-bent on achieving recognition. She was acutely aware of the gap between what is and what could be – never mind what should be – but at the age of 27, she knew that time was definitely still on her side. Patience, focus and perseverance, she intoned like a mantra.

After less than four hours' sleep, Waves was having a hard time concentrating. The effects of the coffee were fading. The warmth of the sun, the uniform throb of the engine and the illusion of little forward movement combined to lull him into a trance. He gazed into the somnolent blue haze, his thoughts wandering: "If we find Champ, my name will be linked with that of

Roland Humphrey, 'The Man Who Discovered Champ.' I'll be famous. Teri Gross will want to interview me. I'll write a book, go on a speaking tour…"

"WATCH OUT!" Roland shouted.

Waves snapped out of his reverie just in time to spin the wheel sharply and swerve around a pontoon boat full of oldsters playing bridge, narrowly avoiding a collision. The Moira's wake rocked their craft. A pitcher of iced tea tipped over and washed away their cards, before sliding off the table and smashing on the deck. An aged card shark shook a bony fist and shouted words inappropriate for the ears of his elderly female companions. "Sorry folks," Waves muttered as they sped away, moving too fast for the card players to have gotten a look at the registration number on the bow, and now too distant to discern the boat's name on the stern. Waves decided it would be best to keep going.

Roland glared at him, then grinned and said, "They should bloody well watch where they're going!"

Waves reduced speed as they drew near enough to discern the island as distinct and separate from the mainland. From a quarter mile away, the rock-girdled mass revealed little more than outer scrub vegetation encircling a dense forest of cedar, spruce and birch. At a distance of 200 yards, he killed the engine.

Jade consulted her laptop. The screen displayed the island and the boat, both surrounded by the moving blotches. "It's beneath us and moving fast. What's our depth?"

"Sixty-two feet," said Waves, checking the digital depth finder on the dashboard. "No wait, now it's 42… 35… and still rising."

Roland leaned over the side and peered into the liquid opacity separating him from whatever was below. "This is most annoying," he said. "We're right on top of something incredible and we can't see a damn thing. Are the scuba tanks charged?"

"Yes, but I don't think it's such a good idea to dive just yet, at least not till we know what we're dealing with," said Waves. "Champ's a carnivore, right? And wouldn't it take a lot of meat to slake his appetite?"

"Yes, theoretically."

"About 170 pounds worth?"

"That ought to do it."

Suddenly a loud squawk emanated from the boat's VHF radio.

"Switch that off," said Roland. "Or at least turn it down."

But before Waves could comply, an irate voice said, "You are approaching private property. Intrusion is prohibited and I will prosecute all trespassers."

Waves grabbed the microphone and said, "And a beautiful day it is too, friend. Who the hell do you think you are, anyway? This isn't the Nevada Testing Grounds and there aren't any nuclear reactors here either."

"I'll deal with this," said Roland. "Hand me the mike... This is Flight Lieutenant Roland Humphrey speaking, a member of her majesty's Royal Air Force. To whom do I have the pleasure of speaking?"

No response.

Finally, after a long pause, the mystery voice replied.

"You must forgive my confrontational tone. I find it necessary to repel the curious and the uninvited. In your case, however, you may proceed to the southeastern tip of my island, where you will enter a narrow inlet. Proceed until you come to a dock, where you can tie your boat. Then follow the path. I will meet you presently."

"You can wipe that smug expression off your face anytime now," said Jade, determined not to let her grandfather bask in his own glory any longer than necessary.

Waves maneuvered the boat around the island at no-wake speed, giving them a chance to gauge its size. "Not much larger than a rugby pitch," said Roland.

Once docked, they followed a narrow path around a table of rock large enough to serve as a sacrificial altar for Druids. Vines and interlocking branches wove above their heads to create a dim, sepulchral atmosphere. They walked on and entered a small clearing amidst the tangled forest, but perceived nothing more than a surrounding wall of trees.

"A deft bit of architecture," said Roland, pointing out the structure that seemed to materialize where none stood a moment before. "All that mirrored glass provides superb camouflage."

A door at ground level swung open. A tall, gaunt figure stepped out and observed them through pale yellow eyes that seldom blinked, missed nothing and conveyed even less.

"Welcome to Dark Island. I am Dr. Stanley Stryker."

The professor shook hands with Roland and said, "After reading of your quest, I knew we were destined to meet."

"This is Jade, my granddaughter and assistant, and Waves, our associate. We had no idea this island was inhabited. It does, in fact, give every indication of being desolate."

"Indeed. It was chosen to provide seclusion and privacy, while still allowing me access to the mainland and the university, where I teach."

"What is your field?" asked Jade.

"Marine biology, although I spend most of my time conducting research. Tell me, what brought you drifting into my waters? Have you found Champ?"

"No, not yet. Although the search for Champ brought us here, we did not drift in. We were attracted."

"Attracted? How interesting. I will hear more. But first, allow me to provide you with a tour and some refreshment." Stryker conducted his guests through the door at ground level, into a spacious chamber whose walls were lined with dozens of stacked aquariums, large and small. "Feel free to examine my collection of pets," he said, before ascending a circular staircase.

The trio marveled at the variety of indigenous and exogenous aquatic life within the aquariums. Roland paused to observe a fat, yard-long eel as it fluttered its dorsal and ventral fins.

Waves peered at a tiny African frog as the transparent little creature sat motionless on the bottom of an aquarium. Suddenly the amphibian kicked to the surface, gulped a breath of air and descended to sit once more on the pebbles.

Their host returned bearing a tray of ice water in tumblers. "Would you believe that little frog is as aware of its corner of the universe as you are?"

"You overestimate me," said Waves. "I have only a worm's-eye view of the universe."

Stryker laughed. "How true. With the exception of dogs, cats, horses and the odd parrot, I've found that most humans have little knowledge or empathy for other forms of life. In fact, their antipathy increases in direct proportion to the organism's xenophobic attributes; the less any given species' head, mouth and eyes resemble their own foolish faces, the greater their contempt... or fear. I have a theory: I strongly suspect that all organisms, even the most diminutive, are exquisitely aware of their respective environments. I also believe that the lower the hierarchy of size and complexity, the more attuned that creature is to its own little niche. Surely, you don't think the forces of evolution were brought solely to bear on the development of our own swollen frontal lobes?"

It was Wave's turn to laugh.

"Go ahead, snicker," said Stryker. "We humans may enjoy dominance on the food chain for the time being, but for countless centuries evolution's great lathe has been honing every living thing on our planet – sharpening their survival skills."

"What, specifically, is your area of specialization?" asked Roland.

"Cartilaginous notochords and all things parasitic," Stryker replied without missing a beat. "And I must admit to deriving a tremendous amount of satisfaction from the knowledge that the parasites of our world all suffer from parasites of their own."

Mad as a bloody hatter, thought Roland.

"So," said Stryker, as if he had just read Roland's mind. "You search for a reptile known to have lived a very long time ago, whereas I devote my energy to species that still exist today. Consider this superb creature for example," he said, directing their attention to the eel in the tank that had previously caught Roland's eye.

"Behold the Asian swamp eel, a truly remarkable species. Not only is it capable of breathing under water or in air, it can alter its gender to allow reproduction in a single-sex environment. When threatened it secretes noxious slime to ward off attacks, although it doesn't have natural enemies. And last but not least, it has no difficulty migrating on land. Adaptive evolution at its most resourceful."

"Your collection is certainly impressive," said Roland, "but there's one species conspicuous in its absence. Why no lamprey?"

"You are an observant individual," said Stryker. "Keeping a lamprey in captivity is difficult. They have very specific thermal and dietary needs and the effort required to fill those needs is simply prohibitive. And besides, as an indigenous species, aren't there enough already out there in the lake?"

Roland found the explanation less than convincing, but held his tongue.

"Earlier, you said that you were attracted to my island. Attracted by what?" asked Stryker.

"See for yourself," said Roland, reaching for the laptop in Jade's shoulder bag. He unzipped it, booted up the machine and typed a command. "As you know, we're conducting our search for Champ using advanced underwater audio technology, coupled with software designed by my granddaughter. Today, our equipment produced the readings that drew us here, but unfortunately, we were misled."

"How so?"

The screen displayed an aerial view of Dark Island, the surrounding waters now clear of the jittering green blotches.

"We picked up anomalous electronic reflections. Nothing real, more's the pity," said Roland, shutting off the computer. "Thank you for an interesting visit, Dr. Stryker. And now, I think we've taken up enough of your time. We really must be off."

"I expect we'll meet again," said Stryker. "Once you've found what you're looking for, or perhaps when it finds you."

The trio exited the glass-walled structure, Roland leading the way as they retraced their steps through the gloomy woods, past the sacrificial cairn and on to the dock. Once onboard, Waves started the engine and guided the Moira through the inlet to open water, and then north.

All three remained silent until the island had receded well into the hazy distance.

"In case you're wondering," said Roland, "I showed the professor a file taken a couple of days ago when I downloaded baseline satellite images of the lake."

"You sly fox," said Jade, as she reactivated her computer. The mysterious blotches reappeared but in far fewer numbers. She watched them disperse, one by one, until only the island remained onscreen. "It's obvious," she concluded. "Whatever produced these images is not a single entity, but a great number of discrete and highly mobile objects."

Chapter Twenty-Two

The next day grew hot, even though the sun lay partially hidden behind a gauzy blanket of cirrus clouds. A pair of sundogs refracted bright patches of prismatic color as Larry Providence stood on the tee of the ninth hole at Rock Cove's golf course – a 300-yard par four with a dogleg into eternity, or so it seemed now that haze obscured the distant green.

In his white silk shirt, baggy slacks and long black ponytail, Larry resembled a debauched samurai who has traded in his sword for a chipping iron. As with all samurai, he sought to perfect his skill and acquire wisdom – the wisdom of holism in one-ism.

Seeking insight, he consulted a folding map outlining the shape of the links. The ninth hole was not only the longest of the 18, but the farthest from the clubhouse. The cup waited on a green amidst a peninsula that jutted into the lake. In addition to the lake's inexhaustible appetite for golf balls, the course also featured a number of small ponds strategically placed to attract – and swallow – them. Many of the ponds were fringed with tall cattails, others with grass. The pond in the middle of the ninth hole connected to the lake via a shallow depression that flooded in the spring and dried up soon thereafter. Normally, only frogs, small fish and water striders inhabited this pond, but now the residents included hungry inhabitants that made the water hazard infinitely more hazardous.

Larry teed up a ball, planted his spiked shoes firmly on the grass and gripped the driver. After one final look in the general direction of the hidden green, he drew back his four-wood and executed a perfect swing. Crack! The ball lofted into the air – a white dot that flew 200 yards before splashing into the pond. Larry muttered a curse as he unwrapped the red cellophane from a new ball. He reinserted the tee and placed the fresh Titleist on the little wooden pedestal's concave crown.

"Eye on the ball… head down… follow through," he chanted before unleashing another towering shot. The ball seemed to accelerate as it hurtled away. The ripples created by the first impact had barely dissipated when the second one bull's eyed the same pernicious body of water.

"May the Scotsman who invented golf roast in hell!" Larry shouted as he flung the driver in disgust. He had long been aware of the game's unlimited potential for frustration, but losing two balls in the same hazard was unprecedented. Larry drew a deep breath to restore his calm, then retrieved his driver and unwrapped another new Titleist.

Sweat trickled from Larry's armpits as he teed up the virgin ball. A third flawless drive propelled it into the sky, but this time it landed on the fairway, bounced twice and rolled to a stop well beyond the water hazard; a good lie for a chip shot onto the green.

"That's more like it," he said as he strode to the cart. The electric motor hummed quietly as he drove off at six miles an hour across the empty acres, leaving behind parallel imprints where the wheels met the grass. Curiosity got the better of Larry Providence as he approached the insatiable pond. He stopped, climbed out and stood at the water's edge.

The pond was circular in shape, with a diameter of approximately 30 feet. Larry looked down and there they were, his new Titleists, lying on the bottom in what looked to be less than three feet of water, practically begging to be retrieved.

"By the ghost of Sam Snead," he declared, "I will not be robbed by a golf course!"

And so, after scanning in all directions, and finding the links empty, Larry stripped off his shirt, slacks, shoes and socks and deposited them in a neatly folded bundle on the cart's seat. Wearing only boxer shorts, he stood and stared at the green-tinged orbs awaiting retrieval. He dipped one foot into the agreeably cool water, and then plunged in like a grizzly going after salmon. The splash produced a miniature tidal wave, the water lapping against the pond's muddy circumference.

Larry held his breath, closed his eyes and submerged. To his surprise, the water was deeper than he had expected – closer to six feet – but it only took a few seconds to grope about and grab the golf balls, one in each hand. A kick stirred up the fine silt and propelled him to the surface, where he tossed the balls onto the grass. But instead of climbing out, Larry floated on his back and enjoyed the impromptu dip. He chuckled at the thought of another golfer coming along to find him wallowing there and wondered what the best explanation might be: "I seem to have lost my ball," although "I seem to have lost my mind" might be more convincing.

High above, a turkey buzzard glided in lazy circles.

Luxuriating in the cool water, Larry became aware of the presence of other living things – a gentle tickling sensation on his back, accompanied by soft feathery touches on his legs. Either the frogs had become bold, he assumed, or inquisitive minnows were nibbling here and there. The tickling sensation grew more pronounced, and then he felt movement against his skin.

"Leeches!" he shouted, rolling over to paddle the short distance to the gently sloping margin. The pressure against his skin increased, accompanied by gentle but insistent suction. If those are leeches, Larry realized, then I'm Arnold Palmer.

Larry bellowed in surprise when incisive teeth punctured the flesh near his shoulder. He reached around, grabbed a lamprey and tore it from his skin, flinging the wriggling creature away; but within seconds every lamprey in the pond had attached themselves to his body with needle-sharp teeth.

The golfer turned skin-diver thrashed the water with both arms as he struggled to reach the edge of the pond. He clawed at the slippery brown muck on hands and knees and tried to stand but the soft mud oozed between his toes and he toppled with a splash. He fought to regain his footing, to reach the grass – and safety – only inches away. But it was not to be.

The lamprey's chisel-tipped tongues jabbed repeatedly, cleaving ever deeper into his flesh, as their digestive enzymes mingled with his blood. The onset of paralysis was swift; within seconds, all volition expired. Every pain receptor in Larry's body erupted in glorious Technicolor, as if hydrochloric acid had replaced every drop of life-giving blood.

Larry's breathing grew shallow as revulsion and disbelief vied with pain. His lips tingled. Helpless rage filled his mind at the realization – he was about to die on a golf course! Not from a heart attack, or cancer or a car crash, but while playing golf!

Warm viscous mud smeared his cheek, clogged his nose and filled his eyes as he slid beneath the surface and sank towards the pond's slimy floor. A feeding frenzy quickly shredded his body, then liquefied and consumed his flesh.

The pond's troubled surface grew placid once more. Turgid water slowly cleared as countless tiny particles of silt drifted down to cover and hide the golfer's gnawed remains.

* * *

Eventually, another ball smacked onto the fairway of the ninth hole, followed shortly after by a duffer driving an electric cart. A second shot brought the seven-stroke handicap player close to the water hazard and it was then he took an interest in the abandoned cart. They were never left out overnight, he knew, because he'd seen the fleet parked at night in a barn near the clubhouse.

"Hello?" he called out.

No response.

How odd, he thought, after finding a neatly folded pair of pants and a silk shirt sitting on the abandoned cart's seat. A pair of socks and spiked shoes waited alongside an expensive set of clubs. Curiosity turned to befuddlement when he noticed two new golf balls lying on the grass a few feet from the edge of the pond's tranquil, reflective ellipse.

Chapter Twenty-Three

The evening silence was unbroken except by rafts of raucous geese congregating out on the lake for an all-nighter. A flock of late arrivals glided overhead as Dot stood by the door, peering out.

"HARVEY!"

The somber woods absorbed her voice. A cardinal's last flight of the day produced a dull, gray streak as Dot slid the door shut and returned to her recliner. Harvey had been gone for hours and she was not accustomed to being on her own.

"At least I'm not alone," she said, glancing at Cricket and Max sprawled nearby on the couch. Come what may, she decided, two dogs and a bottle of vodka can always be relied upon to provide a certain amount of camaraderie. And besides that, she had her pistol.

Cricket stepped off the couch, wagged her tail and barked once.

"Where's Harvey?" asked Dot.

Cricket barked twice more, as if to confirm her awareness of his exact location.

"Yes? Harvey! Cricket, go find Harvey."

Once again she opened the door. Cricket trotted out – moist black nose to the ground – then across the yard and down the path. Once beyond the pool and through the woods, the dog paused atop the metal stairs leading to the lake. Although the sun had set, daylight still lingered in the western sky. Cricket ambled down the steps and stood atop the concrete steps at the waterline.

The surface was unbroken. Wind and waves had not yet swept away the tree pollen's saffron filigree. A doomed black ant rode the surface tension, waving its antennas helplessly as the inexorable current carried it along. Cricket leapt in, oblivious to the ant's plight. Now in the current's grip, she was unaware of the distance to the cement steps, increasing with every passing second. Suddenly the dog comprehended her predicament, and began to swim towards a rocky outcrop, fighting against the current's relentless tug, seeking a place to stand and catch her breath.

Cricket's front paws sought purchase on the slippery wet rocks, but without warning, a lamprey fastened its oral hood onto her belly and tore off a swatch of fur. Cricket yelped as she struggled to climb out of the water.

Another abrupt yank exposed soft, vulnerable skin. She fought against her unseen attacker and managed to climb onto the outcrop. Safe for the moment, the dripping canine stood on a narrow ledge alongside a sheer rock cliff. Realizing there was no escape except by water, she whined for a minute and then leapt back in, only to find that her vigorous paddling merely equaled the speed of the current. The distance to the steps, and safety, remained unchanged.

The lamprey attacked a third time, successfully attaching its oral hood onto unprotected dog flesh. Barking continuously, the spaniel fought in vain against the current and the added weight of the lamprey. The dog quickly grew tired. A moment later, the parasite pulled her under.

* * *

"HARVEY! CRICKET!"

Dot listened but heard only the distant carousing of geese.

"Where could those two have gone?" she wondered. Although Harvey's absence worried her, the missing dog caused greater anxiety. She returned once more to her recliner and sat, drinking screwdrivers and thinking about her estranged mother: Separated by bitterness and animosity as deeply embedded in their psyches as the marrow in their bones, neither woman was inclined to extend the olive branch of reconciliation. It had been years since they had spoken. Not even a Christmas card spanned the gulf.

A warm errant breeze distended the curtains as Dot picked up the phone and dialed the State Police. Sergeant Edwards was on duty and answered the call.

"What can I do for you?" he asked after identifying himself.

"Harvey and Cricket are gone and I'm worried sick. First Sam died and now this!"

"Hold on a minute. Who is Harvey? And who are Cricket and Sam?"

"Sam was one of our dogs; he dropped dead very unexpectedly. Now Cricket is missing, and so is Harvey, my husband."

"When did you last see your husband?"

Dot explained that Harvey had gone outside to work on the pool earlier that afternoon, saying he'd be finished in a couple of hours. "I waited and waited and then it began to get dark, so I let Cricket out to go look for him. And now she's gone too."

"I understand your concern," replied the sergeant, "but it's a bit premature for us to investigate. It's likely your husband and the dog will show up, if not tonight then tomorrow morning."

"Harvey didn't take the van. I never let him go anywhere without me."

"Could he have been picked up by someone else?"

"Not likely. We're here only in the summer and we never socialize."

"You mentioned another dog's death. Tell me about that."

"It was awful! Sam walked in, barfed all over the rug and then dropped dead. Harvey said it was old age but I'm not so sure. Sam was fine until he came back from the lake; his paws were wet so I know he went down to the water."

"Sounds to me like he got into a bloom of toxic algae, which has proliferated to a far greater extent than usual this year. Even a small amount can kill a dog if it's ingested. A veterinarian could perform an autopsy to determine the cause of death."

"Can't. Harvey buried him somewhere in the woods."

"I see. Then there's not much I can do tonight. If your husband has not returned by tomorrow afternoon, call again and we'll take the next step. Till then, try not to worry."

Dot hung up and looked at Max. The spaniel's eyes were fixed steadily upon her. She returned the stare and wondered, was the dog really radiating unconditional positive regard, or something far more pragmatic? Do pets ever size up their owners in terms of lunch, dinner and a midnight snack? She dismissed the thought, bolstered her drink with a splash of vodka, picked up the TV remote and killed an hour channel surfing.

Heeding the call of nature, Dot rose from her recliner. She was not about to use the nearer of the two bathrooms, the site of her sharp prick of inexplicable adversity, so instead she grasped her cane and the leather pistol bag and hobbled to the far end of the house. Once down the steps and into the master bedroom, she walked around the waterbed and up three more steps into the master bath.

The innocuous, mint-green porcelain toilet waited as she unzipped the bag and extracted the Walther. She raised the toilet lid, then held the pistol out and sighted down its blue steel length, aiming – point blank – at the bowl. Suddenly Max bounded up the steps, walked to the fixture and began lapping water from his favorite drinking bowl. "No, Max," she commanded. "Get away from there!"

The dog ignored her.

Her finger tightened inadvertently on the trigger. The hammer fell and the weapon went off with a frighteningly loud bang! The bullet shattered the toilet tank and buried itself in the wall as ten gallons of cold water splashed across the floor. Dot staggered back and dropped the pistol, unsure as to whether she'd shot the dog or not. Max galloped for the stairs, claws skittering wildly, but he collided with and knocked the cane from her grasp.

The woman collapsed – whacking the side of her head on the wall – then fell on her spindly left arm, splintering the radius and the ulna like Popsicle sticks. Stunned and bleeding profusely from a gash on her cheek, she lay amidst sharp porcelain fragments. She sat upright, grasped the Walther in her right hand and watched a lamprey as it slithered up and over the rim of the toilet bowl. Now at eyelevel, the eel opened its oral hood, revealing a repulsive disk full of spiky orange teeth.

Dot raised the Walther's ugly snout and emptied the clip in one deafening, trigger-pulling spasm. The slugs pulverized the bowl, gouged divots in the wall and produced a geyser of water from a shut-off valve that would never again shut off.

"HARVEEEYYY!" she wailed.

On any other day her husband would've heard the shots and come running, but today he was shielded from all noise by the north wall of the house, the intervening woods and the water in the pool, to say nothing of the absolute insularity of death.

Seized by fury, Dot grasped her cane and bludgeoned the lamprey until all that remained was a bloody pulp. She lay back on the floor and groaned as cold water seeped through her clothes and soaked her pink bunny slippers. The pain from her broken arm banished all thoughts of Max as she struggled to her knees and then to her feet.

She tottered to the steps and descended. Suddenly a fragment within the shattered fixture dislodged; the fountain of water became a torrent that cascaded down the steps and across the bedroom floor, expanding outwards like an amoebic psuedopod. But worst of all were the lampreys issuing forth amidst the gushing water. They plopped to the floor, one after another – dozens of slippery coiling eels – all carried forward and down the stairs by the flow.

In shock, Dot staggered to the waterbed, turned and pitched backwards onto its warm, soft surface. She drew her legs up over the side and lost consciousness.

Max ventured out from behind the couch in the living room, looked around cautiously and then approached the master bedroom. The dog descended all three steps, hopped up and stretched out alongside his mistress for a nap, as gallon after gallon of lake-water cascaded from the bathroom.

After an hour, the secondary water pump in the crawlspace beneath the house overheated and seized up, but by then the bedroom was awash in two feet of lamprey-infested water.

Chapter Twenty-Four

The first thing Dot became aware of as she regained consciousness was the sensation of Max's tongue sliding across her cheek, accompanied by the unmistakable smell of dog breath. When she tried to shoo him away with her left hand, daggers of pain struck as unexpectedly as the assassins of Caesar.

"Haaaarrrvveeey," she moaned.

The house remained silent.

Darkness filled the room. Dot groped for the bedside lamp with her right hand, but succeeded only in knocking the vintage rotary dial phone off the end table. A part of her brain registered the incongruous sound of a splash, as opposed to the hard clatter of plastic hitting the wooden floor, but she ignored it. She tried again and this time found the switch and turned on the lamp. A 40-watt bulb revealed the weathered, barn-board walls, the painting of sun-drenched buttes in Arizona, the crimson drapes across both windows and the television mounted on a wall bracket. The room appeared normal from her perspective, supine on the waterbed's pliant surface.

Dot took a deep breath to steel herself against the pain in her arm and a headache that threatened to split her skull. She sat up, swung her legs over the waterbed's side and lowered both feet into cold water.

"Hoooha!" she shouted, withdrawing her legs. But with only one good arm, she was unable to pivot her body. The exertion resulted in radiating waves of agony as the splintered bones in her arm grated against one another; both feet plunged back into the water, the liquid reaching to just below her knees. The lampreys reacted swiftly. Some tore off her bunny slippers, while others began to coil around her ankles. She kicked vigorously, dislodging and flinging them away. One hit the wall with a dull thud and splashed into the little pool that had once been a bedroom.

A numbing horror gripped her mind as she leaned over and peered at the black water. Only two inches of padded wood separated her from the repulsive little fiends.

Looking up briefly, Max heaved a sigh – unaware of his mistress's plight – then settled down again to resume his nap.

Dot knew she must summon help, but did not know how. The telephone lay on the floor – underwater – beyond reach. The bathroom was nearby and she considered jumping to the top step and then climbing out the window; but with the use of only one hand, she doubted her ability to climb through and rejected the idea. Salvation beckoned from the dining room, but several feet of lamprey-infested water lay between the bed and the steps leading up to it.

Out of sheer habit, she picked up the TV remote and switched the set on. A local newscaster appeared in mid-report, saying, "… a busy day on Lake Champlain. The State Police are still searching for two fishermen reported missing. The Coast Guard has reported receiving a record number of calls from people who claimed to have seen Champ, the Lake Champlain monster. And in another lake-related story…"

"Help me!" she pleaded to the reporter's oblivious face.

Dot switched the set off and reached out to return the TV remote to its customary place, but this time she knocked the lamp off the end table. As it hit the water, the bulb exploded, tripping a circuit breaker and plunging the room back into impenetrable night. The woman clenched her teeth and lay as rigid as a corpse, breathing in quick shallow gasps. Only a thread – a wisp of lint – now separated her from panic so primal that only a kicking, screaming tantrum could adequately express it. Eventually she lapsed into a feverish sleep that did not, in any way, knit up the raveled sleeve of care.

But as she slept, the lampreys wriggled up and over the waterbed's sides. The comforter and sheets offered little resistance to their thorn-like teeth and soon the inner mattress lay exposed. Blade-tipped tongues easily punctured the plastic membrane; the warm bacteria-laden water hemorrhaged copiously. Max awoke and leapt nimbly off the bed. He swam the short distance to the steps, clambered up and shook himself free of the lampreys that had not been quick enough to get a firm grip on his short fur.

Dot awoke and opened her eyes. Perceiving only darkness, she was unsure if she were living or dead. All doubt vanished when a lamprey bit into the flaccid muscle of her thigh. Others undulated across the bed's soaked expanse and attached their oral hoods to her torso. They sliced into her flesh with the ease of a shiny new razor blade hewing cheese.

The besieged woman summoned all her remaining strength and channeled it into one final paroxysm of despair – a scream of operatic volume and duration. Max responded with a howl from the dining room as digestive enzymes loaded with neurotoxins entered her bloodstream; the rapid onset of paralysis reduced the scream to a whimper… and then silence.

Dot lay splayed on her back, eyes slewed permanently to the left, mouth gaping in an ugly rictus of torment and fear. Immobilized but conscious, she floated on a boiling lava-lake of pain.

Hell offers no greater epicurean delights than those enjoyed by the lampreys as they feasted on her liquefied muscle tissue. But all during the gruesome banquet, the floodwaters had been slowly draining away through tiny cracks between the floorboards. The lampreys sensed the loss of water and detached their oral hoods, even though plenty of food still remained. They turned away and dropped back into the diminishing depth. Soon, all that remained were dozens of dying lampreys squirming helplessly on the damp floor.

When at last the growing light of dawn began to seep through the crimson curtains, it filled the room with a ruddy glow that revealed the lampreys that had suffocated in the air.

Max trotted nervously from the dining room to the front door, still expecting Harvey to return any minute to feed him. The hungry dog clambered down the stairs into the bedroom, jumped over the side of the deflated waterbed and lay down alongside his paralyzed mistress. Dot clung precariously to life and very much wanted to tell the dog to go and find help, but her body would never again respond to the commands of her brain.

Max licked the salty tears that moistened Dot's cheeks. The sound of slurping grew loud in her ears as the dog swabbed her blood-streaked face with a tongue as pink as a thick slice of ham. When an inadvertent nip from his teeth brought no reaction, he snagged an earlobe, tore off the pinna and swallowed it. Still no protest, so he went after the other ear. These tasty morsels merely whetted Max's appetite. Increasingly ambitious bites stripped the flesh from Dot's cheek, first one and then the other, accompanied by the ripping sound of flesh being torn away – as awful a noise as the bone-conducted sound of wisdom teeth being extracted by a sadistic dentist with a pair of rusty pliers.

Max's head loomed large in her vision – the last thing Dot would ever see – a moment before he pressed his snout beneath her chin and tore out her larynx. The dog crunched the bloody cartilaginous mass once, twice, then swallowed it and went back for more.

Chapter Twenty-Five

Great expanses of woods and pasture still abutted the lake to the north and south of Krampton, a margin delineating secluded coves, inlets and bays. Never-the-less, the public's access to the water shrank as developers bought out retiring farmers, carved the acreage into ever-smaller parcels and built luxury vacation homes for the ultra-rich. Where oaks once spread their limbs, immense houses, many with both indoor and outdoor tennis courts, now stood.

Invariably, the first thing the new owners of these behemoths did was to nail up NO TRESPASSING signs on every remaining tree.

Those unable to afford lakeside property, or even a few days at the Rock Cove Resort, were left with only one alternative – Dead Creek State Park. There, just a few miles from the resort, the park featured campsites and a wide sandy beach bordering a shallow bay. The sluggish river that gave the park its name emptied into the lake nearby, after meandering through miles of bottomland and inaccessible, mosquito-infested forest.

Although Monday afternoon was pleasantly warm, the beach attracted few visitors. Those who flocked in on weekends were now, for the most part, incarcerated in office cubicles, staring blank faced with boredom at computer screens, hawking unwanted commodities over the phone, or performing the innumerable mundane tasks required to keep the gears of commerce grinding.

There were exceptions; a windsurfer enjoying a day of freedom, and Mrs. Margaret Spaulding, accompanied by her creamy-cheeked toddlers, Becky and Leslie, and their neurotic Dachshund, Basil. The dog sat at Mrs. Spaulding's feet, watching the shallow, lapping water with deep suspicion. He had never trusted the lake, for such stubby legs were useless for swimming.

The twins played happily in the warm sand as their mother read a lurid paperback romance. (The cover bore the image of a shaggy-haired hunk with pectorals the size of cinder blocks, cutlass in hand and a swooning wench clasped to his bronzed chest).

Looking up at the conclusion of a particularly torrid chapter, Mrs. Spaulding caught sight of a windsurfer scudding across the lake, out beyond the shallow bay. Propelled by a spanking breeze, booming along at 30 miles an hour, the rider clasped the sail and leaned out over the water's surface.

Every now and then he wiped out, having lost the endless contest between wind and water, and their unruly siblings, inertia and resistance. After each upset he climbed back on and sat astride the board, unaware of having become the target of an intense bioelectric scan conducted by a growing number of lampreys.

His naked feet presented a most alluring target. But by the time the hungry predators ascertained his position and began to close in, he was up and away, tacking swiftly on a new trajectory across the lake's wind-lashed surface.

Mrs. Spaulding returned to her bodice-ripper after a reassuring glance at the twins. Becky and Leslie sat in two inches of warm water, scooping sand with colorful toy shovels as the wavelets lapped at their chubby pink legs.

Basil got up and walked warily along the shore, his pathetic stick of a tail tucked between his hind legs. The dog stepped cautiously into the shallows and lowered his muzzle for a drink.

A lamprey darted towards him, but it was Basil's lucky day, and a quick jump saved him. Thoroughly alarmed, the dog rushed from the beach as fast as his legs would carry him. Mrs. Spaulding noticed the dog's hasty retreat out of the corner of her eye but was not about to get up and chase after him. She turned her gaze once more to her children, who sat giggling and waving their arms. Unlike Basil, they were not afraid of the water.

The Dachshund didn't stop running till he reached the parking lot, at which point Mrs. Spaulding folded a corner of the page, dropped the book onto the sand and heaved herself out of the folding chair. "Basil!" she called. "Come here, poochie!"

The dog did not obey.

Annoyed, Mrs. Spaulding began to walk towards the parking lot, calling out the dog's name. Gurgling with joy, the twins took advantage of their mother's rare lapse of attention and crawled on hands and knees into slightly deeper water, much the way newly hatched sea turtles scurry across the sand towards the safety of the ocean.

No rapacious gulls wheeled overhead, ready to swoop down and pick off the scrabbling little terrapins. Instead, a swarm of lampreys entered the shallows and rapidly closed the gap separating them from the toddlers.

Only a minute had elapsed before Mrs. Spaulding heard an alarming cry.

A minute can be a very long time indeed, and this particular minute would haunt the poor woman for the rest of her life. For there, already 20 feet beyond the dry sand of the beach, moving swiftly into deeper water, she saw a coiling, brown mass dragging her children away.

Mrs. Spaulding's scream did not reach the ears of the park lifeguard that morning – he was not scheduled to swab his nose with white sunscreen and sit atop the lookout chair till Friday. It did, however, rouse the college kid dozing in the booth at the entrance to the parking lot.

Still screaming, Mrs. Spaulding ran across the sand and into ankle deep water, which grew deeper with each step, but each one brought her no closer to her children. Powerless against the combined strength of the lampreys, the twin's voices grew to shrill, keening screeches until the swarm pulled them under, abruptly squelching their cries.

The silence, however brief, was deafening.

The sound of Mrs. Spaulding's shrieking quickly filled the void as she waded into deeper water, now at her knees. Lampreys veered towards her. She felt their slippery embrace as several entwined about her calves. Sobbing hysterically, Mrs. Spaulding kicked her feet, dislodged the lampreys before they could bite and hurried away, back onto dry sand.

A moment later the park employee ran up and said, "What happened?"

"My children," she gasped between sobs, "They're gone!"

Chapter Twenty-Six

The cruiser's blue lights flashed as Sergeant Edwards prepared to ticket the out-of-state Jetta he'd just pulled over for exceeding the speed limit. He paused, pen in hand, as the dispatcher's voice on the radio directed him to Dead Creek State Park – at once – to investigate a possible drowning.

"On my way," he replied, before letting the offending but suitably contrite driver off with a warning. After executing a swift U-turn, he sped north on Route 7, the blue lights still flashing.

Paul Edwards was by no means the only officer assigned to the rural precinct that included Krampton, but lately, the lake had become his primary beat. The usual fender-benders, domestic disputes, vandalism and burglaries now struck him as piddling infractions compared to the mystery posed by the still growing list of water-related fatalities. How, he wondered, could anyone drown at a beach where the sand sloped away so gradually the water remained shallow for hundreds of feet?

Trouble at the park was rare. College kids drinking beer and raising hell while campers tried to sleep… a skunk-blast at close range… that was about the extent of it.

Until today.

The landmark indicating the turn onto the access road was impossible to miss: In blatant defiance of the state's no-billboard law, a large sign displayed the names of all who claimed, at one time or another, to have seen Champ, the fabled Lake Champlain monster. Samuel de Champlain topped the list – the first European to set eyes on the lake 400 years ago, and reputed to have glimpsed its most elusive denizen. The most recent name added was that of Agnes Pacquette (who, if the true were known, would much rather have seen a manifestation of the Virgin Mary's face in the mold stain on her bathroom wall).

The access road wound for six miles, at times running alongside the sluggish brown waters of Dead Creek, before terminating at the park's entrance, where a yellow sign with black letters advised,

CAUTION – MONSTER XING

The sergeant pulled into the parking lot, climbed out of the cruiser and walked towards the only two people on the beach: A distraught, hysterical woman, and a park employee, who quickly related what little information he could. "She arrived in a Volvo station wagon with two children and a dog, about an hour ago. They sat on the beach, everything was fine and that's all I know."

Mrs. Spaulding muttered and sobbed as she glared at the water like a moon-struck zombie. She turned her swollen, tear-streaked face to the officer, pointed to the bay and said, "Water snakes took my children." The enormity of her loss evoked additional wrenching sobs.

"Take her to my cruiser," Edwards told the park employee, "while I look around."

"No!" she shrieked. "My babies are still out there."

"We'll do everything possible to find your children," he assured her. "In a while I'll take you home, or better yet, to a friend's house, if your husband is working. You shouldn't be alone and I don't want you behind the wheel. I'll make sure your vehicle is returned."

Suddenly a small brown animal scampered across the field towards them.

"Basil!" cried Mrs. Spaulding, scooping up the squirming Dachshund and holding him tightly in her arms. The dog licked her face and gave its little tail a wag. The parking attendant gently ushered her away. Edwards kneeled to examine the indentations in the sand surrounding a folding chair, too indistinct to be called footprints. Nearby, a paperback and a couple of small plastic shovels lay on the sand – nothing to substantiate the mother's claim except her very real anguish.

What did the woman mean by "water snakes," he wondered? Are there water snakes in Lake Champlain? Hagfish, perhaps, they feed en mass, but the officer felt sure hagfish were strictly ocean dwellers. Edwards was aware of the ongoing attempts to control the lamprey infestation, and he recalled the wildlife officers killed while working to control them, but it didn't make any sense, lamprey attacks against people were rare. A long-distance swimmer might encounter one, but only if they'd been in the water long enough to substantially lower their skin temperature. And certainly, he knew of no such attacks conducted by more than one, and never in warm shallow water.

Edwards sought in vain for any element – other than the lake itself – that might link this latest event to those before. Although the beach looked tranquil and inviting, it was the scene of yet another inexplicable tragedy.

There were no similarities except for the complete lack of substantive evidence.

* * *

An immaculate teal and mauve van stuffed with electronics and a television news-team from Channel Three pulled into the parking lot. A boom-mounted parabolic antenna extended upwards from the vehicle's roof, then tilted into optimum alignment with the satellite that connected it to the home studio in Burlington. There, someone monitored police radio frequencies, ready to dispatch the mobile unit whenever they caught wind of an unfolding true-life drama likely to attract viewers, or more importantly, increase advertising revenue.

An attractive brunette hopped out of the van. She wore a business suit, too much make-up and a toothy, often fraudulent smile oddly reminiscent of the radiator grill on a '58 Buick. Although the reporter harbored delusions of significance, she specialized in puff pieces – flower shows, cat shows, or getting opinions from pedestrians on the street about matters they knew little or nothing about. It had been a lucky coincidence that she and her team were nearby when the dispatch came through. Like most small-town television personalities, she yearned to be taken seriously as a journalist and to make the jump someday from the boondocks to the big time.

The sergeant watched as the news team prepared to roll tape. He considered the broadcast of grief a vulgar encroachment on the privacy of the bereaved. And so, he was not about to allow them anywhere near Mrs. Spaulding. Instead, the reporter questioned the park employee as the cameraman set up a tripod on the beach. Anything is better than nothing, thought the technician as he shot footage of the lake using a slow, left to right pan. The images would be spliced in later to add bulk to a story that had yet to reveal anything solid enough to be called newsworthy.

"Ready when you are, Kimberly," said the cameraman as the reporter applied a fresh layer of makeup to her face, a practice he regarded as embalming the living.

Kimberly held the microphone near her chin, looked directly into the lens and began.

"We're live in Krampton, at the water's edge in Dead Creek State Park, to investigate the sudden disappearance of two small children. Details are sketchy, but it is feared they may have drowned. If so, this brings the recent death toll in this tranquil lakeside community to a total of six. We do not yet know the cause, some may be accidental but others are extremely questionable."

Just then the windsurfer rounded the point, traversed the mouth of the bay and entered the camera's field of view, alongside Kimberly's talking head. The videographer recognized another potentially useful scrap of footage and zoomed in on the surfer's ride across the wind-spanked surface.

And then something else caught his eye – a disturbance in the water, a long way off, but directly behind the windsurfer. He zoomed in as close as his lens would allow but the source of the disturbance remained unclear. It wasn't a boat wake, although it moved like one. The reporter realized that she was no longer the center of attention, turned to look and asked, "What've you got?"

"I don't know. It's too far away to make out. Wait, it's gone… no, it's back again. It rises and falls as if it were submerging and resurfacing."

"Keep rolling," she said. "We'll go with a possible Champ sighting."

They watched the intriguing surface activity as it receded and disappeared. Too distant to identify, the sighting would nevertheless become the happy-news alternative to the day's big story, the tragic disappearance of the Spaulding twins.

Chapter Twenty-Seven

Snee awoke the following morning after eight hours of dream-polluted sleep. He crawled out of his mildew-dampened tent and squinted at a sky as featureless as brushed aluminum, and then at the lake, its surface covered with moving oval patterns that expanded and shrank with restless energy.

"Breakfast is the most important meal of the day," he muttered, opening a can of sardines and slapping the headless oily corpses between two slices of stale white bread.

Something in the water caught his eye as he sat munching.

There, less than a hundred feet away, moving perpendicular to the shore, a large V-shaped wake rippled closer. Snee stopped chewing when four dark, fleshy mounds breached the surface, each about a yard long, and each separated by five or six feet of water.

"Chump's humps flackering in the ovoids!" he declared.

Snee watched intently as the dark objects continued on a northerly course in single file, moving silently and swiftly until the fir trees hid them from view. A moment later the fourth hump in line submerged, only to reappear directly alongside the third. As good a view of Champ as anyone would ever get, each moving shape was nothing more than the glistening back of a migrating sturgeon.

Snee concluded breakfast with an apple to cleanse his remaining teeth. Then he climbed the steep hillside and warily approached his bicycle, hidden in the bushes. No sign of the dogs as he stepped quietly onto the road, determined to visit the store and share his eyewitness account of Champ.

A minute later, Sergeant Edwards sped by in his cruiser, enveloping Snee in a cloud of dust and disoriented grasshoppers. The officer arrived at the store, parked out front and entered.

"Hello Paul," said Howard. "I just heard the latest, on the scanner. Any sign of the twins yet?"

"No, Howard, it's much too soon. Our divers are still en route. But I expect the TV news people will hover like vultures. What's new around here? Anything I should know about? You are, after all, my eyes and ears in the wilderness."

"Nothing new to report from this end of the string. Folks are unsettled by all the terrible news coming out of our little town lately. What with all the rain and bad publicity, the tourists aren't flocking in. I'm not selling much of anything except ammo, more than ever before in fact. Everyone's so jumpy they're locking their doors at night for the first time ever."

"Not a bad idea. You never know who might try to get in."

"Who or what. Marion and Abe were here yesterday and they're still arguing over who'll pay for the damage when his cows ran wild and paid her a little visit."

"I'm ready for some soft news. What happened?"

"No one knows why, but Abe's entire herd went crazy and broke through a wall to get out of the barn – kicked it to pieces – have you ever heard the like? They stampeded up and down the road and a bunch of 'em got onto Marion's deck. They trampled her potted plants and now she's holding him responsible."

"That is odd. A cow getting loose and wandering off is common, but not the entire herd. I suppose we'll never know what goes on in a cow's head. Speaking of odd, what can you tell me about Professor Stryker?"

"I doubt we'll ever know what goes on in his head either," said Howard. "The professor keeps to himself. Doesn't come into the store more than once or twice a year; doesn't belong to any civic organizations or clubs and he's never been to church as far as I know. Spends all his time on that island of his or at the university."

"Have you seen his wife lately?"

"No, come to think of it. She used to stop in from time to time, but she hasn't in a while."

"I'd like to talk to her, but no one seems to know where she is."

"I'll see what I can dig up," Howard promised.

Just then the door opened and in walked Rock Cove's general manager.

"Hello Elsbeth," said the sergeant. "I was just on my way to see you."

"In that case," she replied, "we should step outside to talk."

Howard chafed at the thought of the best gossip of the day about to transpire just beyond earshot. But a moment later he heard Elsbeth's voice loud and clear . . .

"Cancel the Fourth of July festivities?" she snorted incredulously. "The idea is preposterous."

"I understand your concerns," replied the sergeant.

"I doubt it."

Howard edged closer to the screen door, convinced the ensuing conversation would be too good to miss. Then he pretended to adjust some items on a shelf.

"Elsbeth, I have reason to believe your guests are in grave danger."

"We've been through all this before, sergeant. In danger from what?"

"Something – and we still don't know what – but something is killing people either on or near the lake. Two small children are missing at Dead Creek State Park, not more than two miles from the resort. And surely you haven't forgotten Thaddeus, or the Jet Skier, or the Wildlife agents? Or the two fishermen that disappeared on opening day of the Fishing Derby? These incidents may look like accidents, but they're not."

"Sergeant, just because a couple of inebriated fools with fishing rods disappear doesn't mean the lake is any more dangerous than usual. A Jet Ski is an open invitation for trouble, which is precisely why we don't allow them at Rock Cove. None of these irritating events is sufficient cause for me to alter our plans to celebrate the Fourth. This will be our hundred-year anniversary and we're going all out. We're having a Champ Day celebration, live music, an art show, fireworks and a special surprise. If we cancelled the festivities, our guests would head right over to Saranac Lake."

"Elsbeth, you're beginning to remind me of an obstreperous goose. You'll go to any length to protect your precious goslings, even if it means endangering the public."

Howard stifled a chuckle.

Elsbeth glared at the sergeant. "Is that so? If I'm a goose then you're a meddling nuisance! Really, the very notion of canceling the celebration is ludicrous."

"You could reschedule it, after we've figured out what's going on."

"Cancellation is out of the question! We've never once skipped the Fourth in all our long history – not even during World War Two – and we're not about to start now. Sergeant Edwards, I'm determined to keep Rock Cove's name unsullied and synonymous with gracious vacation living."

"Is that what you call it? What about gracious vacation dying? The details concerning the death of the Wildlife agents have been withheld from the public, although suppressed would be more accurate, but you and I know better."

"So? That in no way affects my decision."

"Elsbeth, imagine for a moment what would happen if my warnings went unheeded and, as a result, one of your guests was hurt or killed. The lawsuits would be staggering. Especially after word got out that you'd been warned of a possible risk all along. And believe me, the word would get out."

"Now who's using blackmail?"

"I understand your current financial strain, but if you go ahead with your plans and something bad happened – forget bankruptcy – you could kiss it all good-bye. As it stands, I don't have the authority to compel you to cancel the celebration, but I strongly urge you to reconsider."

"I appreciate your candor, sergeant, but I've heard nothing to convince me of the need for such a drastic step. Before I'd even consider it, I'd have to personally observe a crocodile swallowing children like snack cakes."

"One last question, Elsbeth. You have a child of your own, correct?"

"Yes, a ten-year old boy."

"Does he like to swim or go fishing in the lake?"

She paused for a moment . . . "Thank you for your concern, sergeant, but you exceeded your 'last question' by two. And now, you must excuse me; I have a lot of work to do. I trust you will keep me informed if anything new . . . ah, surfaces."

Elsbeth ascended the store's front steps and paused just long enough to give Howard the opportunity to hastily abandon his listening post.

"Tell me, sergeant, Rock Cove's Independence Day celebration is coming up soon. Will you be attending as a spectator or as a police officer?"

"That remains to be seen."

Chapter Twenty-Eight

The power company's meter-reader enjoyed her job, especially in July when birds trilled, gentle zephyrs caressed every leaf and the scent of countless blooms filled the air with heavenly fragrance. A spectacular day was in progress as she made her way from one domicile to the next, peering at the little dials in each meter and jotting down the numbers that indicated the amount of electricity used since her last inspection. The woman opened the gate and walked across Harvey and Dot's spacious lawn, but in spite of the perfumed air, she detected the unmistakable stench of death.

The concerned meter-reader poked around the yard just long enough to determine that the reek was not the result of a dead possum or some other animal decomposing amongst the leaf litter. No, she decided, the smell definitely grew stronger as she neared the house. Not much electricity used, she noted after a look at the meter on an outside wall. The woman spoke to her home office via the radio in her vehicle and they, in turn, called the State Police.

Sergeant Edwards received a transmission from headquarters as he drove east, away from Krampton. He acknowledged his instructions and said, "That town is becoming a genuine pain in the neck." The officer recalled the conversation a week ago with the woman worried about her missing spouse. She never called back and he'd assumed all was well.

And now this.

Ten minutes later Edwards parked his green and gold cruiser at the gate leading to Harvey and Dot's summerhouse. One glance at the roadside mailbox overflowing with bills, magazines and junk mail aroused his suspicions. He opened the gate, walked across a lawn in need of cutting and approached the house.

"State Police," he announced in a loud voice, peering through the glass into the dim living room and knocking on the door with his knuckles. "Anyone home?"

No answer, so he slid the door open and stepped in. The nauseating smell of putrefaction immediately assaulted him. He gagged and quickly covered his nose and mouth with a handkerchief. Shutting the door behind him out of sheer habit, he drew his flashlight and began to search an interior made dim by dark paneling on the walls and thick brown drapes covering the windows.

The smell grew stronger as he ventured deeper into the house. His eyes watered as he stepped around numerous fecal sausages littering the floor – some desiccated, others moist – all contributing to the unholy, nauseating stench. The officer's search of the living room and kitchen revealed nothing, both were empty, as was the dining room.

Pausing at the top of three steps leading down to the master bedroom, Sergeant Edwards shined his light into a five-star hotel-room from hell – a chamber of horrors glowing crimson from the sanguineous daylight seeping through heavy scarlet drapes. He nearly vomited, for there, stretched out on a waterbed, a gnawed female corpse lay incandescent with putrescence.

Pale, writhing maggots fell from empty eye sockets and filled the gaping oral cavity as their older siblings buzzed languidly through the noisome air.

The recumbent form still clutched a TV remote in one bony hand, as if death itself could not preempt the soap operas. Matted, disheveled blond hair hung limply from the mottled scalp of this Breck girl from the pit, an image that would haunt the sergeant's memory for a long time – but the worst sight of all was the dog crouching alongside.

Max glared silently at the intruder with teeth bared and eyes brimming with insanity.

"There's a good dog," the sergeant said in a gentle, placating tone of voice.

Max began to growl.

The officer unsnapped the safety strap on his holster and aimed his flashlight into the Spaniel's eyes as he slowly backed away. Still chewing on a grizzly morsel, Max upped the ante with a deeper growl. Edwards backed steadily through the dining room and into the kitchen, where an idea occurred to him. Opening a low cupboard, he located a bag of dog chow and filled a bowl with nuggets, then placed it on the floor.

"Good dog," he said, continuing his slow, careful retreat.

Max stepped off his mistress' bier, climbed the three steps and entered the dining room. The spaniel exhibited the hangdog demeanor of a dog that knows it has been a very bad dog indeed. He sniffed the offering and snorted an unequivocal rejection.

Never again would he be content to eat mere Alpo.

The officer continued his retreat, moving through the living room without once taking his eyes off the dog. Max followed, head held low, snarling ominously. Edwards now stood with his back against the glass door, flashlight in one hand and service revolver in the other.

He almost escaped unscathed, but for one critical mistake: Seeking the door handle, he glanced away for an instant, and in that split second Max leapt for his throat. Edwards fired at the moving blur – spattering the wall with gray matter dog brains. Dead in mid-air, Max struck him on the chest and together they fell, shattering the glass and tumbling out onto the grass.

The trooper rolled the canine with the ruined head off his chest and groaned as he rose to his feet. Unhurt except for a few minor cuts, and more importantly – unbitten – the cruiser's first-aid kit provided disinfectant for his wounds, plus a roll of gauze and surgical tape.

Unfortunately, Sergeant Edward's duty was not done for the day, in spite of the afternoon's demonstrably ferocious temperament, for he knew the entire estate must now be searched.

Edwards traversed the yard, looking first in the empty barn before following the path through the woods to the steps that descended to the lake. He found nothing unusual and returned. But as he skirted the pool, he noticed something odd about the water and paused... it was not the sparkling cobalt blue typical of backyard pools, but a dull, scummy green.

A pool to kill your appetite for swimming, he thought as he walked on, unaware that it was a pool with an appetite of its own. For, hidden beneath its bilious surface, numerous lampreys rested, hidden amongst a dun carpet of dead leaves and human bones.

Although the lampreys were trapped, they had fed well and could survive captivity for a long time. Eventually, someone would come along and feed them.

Chapter Twenty-Nine

At last, the big day arrived. The Fourth dawned sultry. Not a leaf stirred in the oppressive air. And although the weather forecast called for the three H's – hazy, hot and humid – it made no mention of rain.

The nub of a turtle's head poked above the lake's surface. The amphibian scrutinized the world through acute yellow eyes until the growing thrum of the Moira's engine alarmed it. One swipe of its exquisitely hydrodynamic limbs sent it curveting into deep water.

"I'd join you if I could," said Waves, "but as I mentioned before, I have two gigs today. We're playing for a cruise this afternoon and then later at the resort."

"It's those bloody squirrels again," said Roland. "But no matter, Jade is an accomplished seaman, or sea woman. With your consent, she will pilot the Moira today."

"I have no objection. The boat's gassed up, the scuba tanks have been refilled and the refrigerator is stocked as per your instructions. You'll find navigational charts in the galley, which I doubt you'll need, and you can always use channel 16 on the radio if you run into trouble."

"What could go wrong?" asked Jade. "It's going to be a fabulous day, with plenty of humidity, which I love. My grandfather can be Neptune and I'll be a mermaid."

"You'd make a better siren," said Waves, "luring innocent sailors to their doom on the rocks."

"There's no such thing as an innocent sailor," said Roland.

She responded with a knowing smile.

"Jade, you have the bridge," said Waves, relinquishing the captain's chair. "And now, I need to be ferried across to the Westport Marina to rendezvous with my ride to the first gig."

Jade scanned the cockpit's gauges and tried to imagine navigation back in the days when ships teetered off the edge of the world, a time when the phrase 'Here there be Dragons' demarcated the limits of cartography.

A short while later she maneuvered the boat into the marina and alongside the floating dock.

"There's just one thing," said Waves. "If Champ shows up, be sure to get a good photograph. Or better yet, drag the damn thing in on a leash."

Just then, a disreputable looking, rust-bitten Chevy van pulled into the marina's parking lot. The van's rear windows were plastered with decals from a dozen famous, big-time rock bands and a small metal plate attached to the front fender exhorted all to "ARRIVE STONED."

"That's my ride," said Waves. "I'll see you tonight at the resort after our show. Good hunting, tally ho and all that." He walked to the van, climbed in and sat amidst a stack of electronic equipment.

After the van drove away, Jade consulted the navigational charts while Roland trained his binoculars on an osprey hovering high above the lake. The raptor hung motionless, scanning . . . then folded its wings, plummeted and struck – impaling a very surprised fish with its powerful talons. The osprey flapped vigorously to gain altitude, then flew off with its catch, dinner for one and a brief, albeit spectacular new perspective for the other.

"It's time we took a closer look at Stryker's island," said Roland. "But first, let's see what your computer has to say, shall we?"

Jade booted up the laptop. "Nothing to report," she said. "The coast is clear."

She steered the boat on a southeasterly heading and watched as the compass swiveled beneath its clear plastic dome. Sealed in liquid, the instrument harkened back to a time when the magnetic properties of a needle were sufficient for navigation, long before the microchip came onboard.

* * *

Sergeant Edwards arrived at Rock Cove along with a steady influx of visitors. The resort remained sacrosanct except on Independence Day, the one day when locals were allowed in to mingle with the gentry. Humidity blanketed everything and everyone and clung like itchy woolen long johns. The officer nodded to a team of rent-a-cops sweltering in the merciless heat, sweat dampening their armpits as they directed arriving traffic onto a mown hayfield, now a parking lot.

Edwards was determined to remain vigilant. An underwater search of the bay at Dead Creek State Park had revealed nothing – no trace of the missing twins had been found. The officer felt a nagging twinge of anxiety and hoped the bustle and commotion of the day's festivities would eradicate the dreadful image of Max's last meal still lingering in his mind's eye.

The observance of Champ Day was well underway and the trooper smiled when a gaggle of children disguised as fledgling sea-monsters paraded across the resort's manicured lawn. Elsbeth emerged briefly from the dining hall to issue instructions to her staff, and they in turn conveyed the orders to a small army of college students indentured till classes began again in the fall.

Nearby, a lawn-sale beckoned; tables were laden with fudge, pies, cookies and an assortment of earnest but hideous little paintings of the lake at sunset – to say nothing of the hand-carved duck decoys, rubber snakes and plastic spiders. Hopeful browsers examined birdcages, 8-track tapes recorded by Perry Como, Jim Nabors and The Ray Coniff Singers, as well as retired CB radios atop dusty stacks of National Geographic back-issues. Someone examined an acoustic guitar with a warped neck, confident the search would eventually reveal an attic Stradivarius or a basement Les Paul.

The sergeant heard strange sounds invading the air, as if a multitude of red-eyed cicadas had just emerged from their 17-year hiatus to buzz the national anthem in unison. A sign tacked to a tree said, "The Krampton Kitchen Band." "Aha," he said after spotting a drove of ancient blue-haired biddies seated on the dining hall's spacious porch, each one playing a kazoo.

Tremulous chords from a vintage Emmanee Electric Organ provided the harmonic glue that kept the kazoo players more or less in the same ballpark, as they played tunes written when Rudi Vallee sang through a megaphone. The ensemble's leader, and only male, was a wiry old rooster who pounded on bongo drums while keeping an eye on his flock.

An incredulous, sullen teenager sat listening, a silent boom-box at his feet. The kid shook his head in disgust as if to say, "What is this god-awful noise? Everyone knows Def Leppard rules." When the Kitchen Band paused for an intermission, the teenager sighed with relief and pushed the button marked "PLAY."

Officer Edwards nodded a greeting to Marion Witherspoon as she sat in the shade, scowling at the violent shift in music. She nodded back and very much wanted to pump him for news, but didn't get the chance. He walked on, aware that he was witnessing a quintessentially rural celebration – an event as unabashedly American as frozen apple pie or an unwed mother.

Nearby, an onslaught of humanity ambled across the resort's lawn. Some carried folding lawn chairs like leaf-cutter ants toting snips of vegetation. Others hefted coolers stuffed with sandwiches and soda. Each arriving family staked out its turf by spreading a blanket on the grass. Infants lay on their backs gurgling as older children ran by, their heads garlanded with plastic haloes that would later glow purple or red in the dark.

Live music greeted visitors at every turn. A throng of tuba players milled about like a herd of shiny golden hippos. After reinforcement with flutes, trombones, trumpets and clarinets, the Winooski Winds played one indefatigable Souza march after another.

The musical piece de resistance – the touted big surprise – was scheduled to arrive onboard a vessel resurrected after many decades of dry-dock retirement at the Shelburne Museum. The venerable Ticonderoga had been re-floated after a decision to generate revenue via "historic" sightseeing cruises. Not a maiden voyage, but an old maid's voyage, the Green Mountain Philharmonic was scheduled to float majestically into the cove at dusk and play a concert on the ship's stately deck, just prior to the fireworks.

Squibs exploded in crackling bursts reminiscent of small arms fire as Sergeant Edwards walked to the tip of the narrow rock peninsula that formed an enclosing arm of the cove. There, professional fireworks technicians worked within a cordoned-off area, preparing dozens of rockets and ground-displays, their fuses waiting only for darkness and the touch of a burning flare.

* * *

Dressed in his least-tattered raiment, Tom Snee was among the teeming throng that surged onto the grounds. He leaned his bicycle against a tree and then infiltrated the old wooden building that housed Rock Cove's annual art exhibition. He cast a critical eye around the walls.

"Well, looky here," he blurted. "Alfred Beirstadt meets Bob Ross! Pure, absolute schlock, but schlock of the very highest order!" He moved on, frowning as he examined painting after painting.

"I could puke," he groaned. "But not on an empty stomach."

The undernourished artist descended upon the buffet table like a lean gray wolf entering a chicken coop. He ignored the white wine but tore off a large hunk of French bread, carpeted it with an inch-thick slab of Brie and took a ravenous bite. Then he reached out a paw, grasped a cluster of grapes and stuffed them into a pocket, then repeated the procedure, filling the other pocket with chocolate-dipped strawberries. "I'll stay at the dinner table just as long as there's something to eat," he muttered after catching sight of a particularly anemic watercolor.

Snee resumed his tour of the art exhibit and wondered why so many painters were timid and afraid of color. And why must they go on painting still more trees, decade after decade, he wondered? A subject as hackneyed as dogs playing poker or Elvis on black velvet.

"What is this ragamuffin doing here?" asked an imperiously overweight guest resplendent in black tie, tails and scarlet cummerbund.

Snee spun around to confront the offended connoisseur of fine art.

"I'm an art cricket, don't ya' you know. Consider this appalling eyesore," he said, indicating a painting choked by the roseate saccharine glow of nostalgia – a rustic cottage smothered in flowers, its roof thatched with sentimentality, Alpine peaks looming in the distance and a parade of unspeakably adorable ducklings waddling past an Adirondack chair in the foreground. "Ever see so many clichés in one frame?" he asked.

"That's one of my paintings," said the man with haughty, magisterial dignity.

"Izzatso? Then I award you first prize for insignificance!" said Snee.

"My paintings are in collections all over the world, you wretched guttersnipe."

Alerted by an observant member of the staff, Elsbeth strode into the gallery.

"Keep your opinions to yourself," she commanded.

"Imelda," he yelped. "What an unpleasant surprise."

"My name is not Imelda," she said, scowling at him from beneath her conch-shell-shaped hairdo. This was not the first time she'd encountered Snee. Accustomed to governing her little kingdom with the totalitarian hegemony last seen during the reign of Queen Victoria, Elsbeth was determined to shepherd this perennial pest away from the exhibition as quickly as possible.

"Crap, Imelda, all crap," he said, gesturing about. "Where are my paintings?"

"If you submitted slides like our featured artists, perhaps the jury would look favorably on your work for next year."

"In a cow's eye they would," he said, spitting a fleck of cheese into the air. "You know, I once read that Vermont's 'sposed to be just ducky for the arts. But what they didn't say was, 'Unless you're an artist, and then, ha-ha, you're screwed!'"

Elsbeth took the shabby upstart firmly by the elbow and hustled him towards the door. The last thing he heard on the way out was a triumphant cry from a matron of the arts who proclaimed, "I'll take all three!"

"Don't do it, lady!" shouted Snee. "It's garbage… effluent!"

Elsbeth dragged him outside, pointed a finger and said, "See that field? There's going to be a rock band playing there soon. Later there'll be fireworks and a big surprise. Go!"

Chapter Thirty

Waves stood on the edge of the pier watching petroleum droplets expand into iridescent amoebas on the lake's glassy surface. Nearby, the Jupiter tugged gently at the hemp lines that tied the old barge to the shore. Now a party boat, her deck would soon fill with day-trippers intent upon an excursion augmented by food, beer and live music provided by Squirrels in the Attic.

All week, radio ads had described the event as a "blues cruise," but the ticket-holders all thought of it as a "booze cruise."

Revelers began arriving as Captain Elmo sat at the Jupiter's bar with Charlie, the leader of the band and its vocalist. Charlie was a genuine rock 'n' roll barbarian with a red beard and ponytail and a tiny globe of the Earth dangling sarcastically from one earlobe. He wore a tie-dyed shirt, jeans and sunglasses; a leather bandoleer filled with harmonicas crossed his scrawny chest – a dozen blues harps that shone like chrome-plated, 50-caliber bullets.

As corpulent as a Sumo wrestler, the captain of the Jupiter wore white shorts and a white shirt with epaulettes, plus a cap festooned with gold embroidery on its visor. An enormous white handlebar mustache drooped below a prominent nose, a beak that cleaved the air like the prow of a ship.

"I'll tell you what they should do," said Charlie. "Every time the NRA elects a new president, someone should step up and shoot 'em. That's right, shoot 'em and keep shootin' till those bozos get the message!"

"No, no, no," replied Captain Elmo. "I admit your suggestion has elegant simplicity and a measure of poetic justice, but the NRA is the last bunch of zealots you want to piss off. Although, come to think of it, you could put one right between the eyes of what's his name, Moses."

"When they wrote the Constitution," Charlie continued, "there were mountain lions and murderous savages behind every bush. You needed guns. Now, 200 friggin' years later, the Indians own gambling casinos, the so-called sportsmen tote semi-automatic rifles and nobody's safe. Last fall some guy was sitting in his living room watching football on TV when a bullet ripped through the wall and killed him."

Captain Elmo looked at his watch. "I'm wanted on the bridge," he said, as if in command of the starship Enterprise and not a rusty bilge-bucket on Lake Champlain. The captain drained his mug, abandoned his stool and then hoisted himself up a ladder to the window-enclosed cockpit. There, he poured a tot of rum from his private stock.

Charlie decided it was time for a sound check. The band's equipment had been assembled under an awning; the amps, monitor speakers, microphones, electric guitars and an electric keyboard were all strung together with lengths of black wire. A set of drums occupied center stage and two hefty PA speakers were held six feet aloft on tripods on either side. Charlie cupped a harmonica and a microphone in his hands and blew a note that sounded like the wail of a banshee. Satisfied with the shriek, he joined the musicians standing at the rail.

"Roll out the red carpet," said Charlie as he watched the approach of their most loyal fan. A guy with long greasy hair, dark circles under his eyes and a flabby stomach beneath a Black Sabbath T-shirt shambled across the gangplank.

"Greetings my fellow Squirrels," said the new arrival. "I'm the Globster and I'm screwed."

"Don't listen to him," said Charlie. "He's having a triple bio-rhythm slump."

"That's right. My girlfriend just dumped me, my mom wants me to get a job and move out of the house. I tell 'ya, it's a real crisis."

Charlie cackled with unsympathetic glee.

"Go ahead, laugh. See if I care."

TR, short for Tabla Rasta, the band's dreadlock-draped Jamaican drummer, gazed at the colossal cauliflower-shaped thunderheads rising high into the sky.

"Them be Caribbean clouds, mon."

"I wouldn't worry about the weather," said Charlie. "You can swim, right?"

"Yeah mon, I spend my entire childhood underwater."

Captain Elmo was also aware of the gathering energy in the sky as he downed the rum, poured another shot and tuned the radio to NOAH weather. A computer-synthesized voice said, "Hayzee sun, humidity and a chance of a shower. Winds at light speed."

"Quite a gale," thought the captain, tossing back another shot. "A hundred and eighty six thousand miles a second!"

On deck, the Globster extracted a small hand-carved pipe from a pocket. "Hey Charlie, look at this; it's my own personal evil spirit." Shaped like a gnome's head, the pipe had a pointed chin, a protuberant nose and flecks of glittering mica for eyes. The Globster filled the cavity in the gnome's head with resinous marijuana buds and torched them with a Zippo lighter old enough to have stormed the beach at Iwo Jima. He inhaled deeply and handed the frothing devil pipe to Charlie.

The head Squirrel took a toke and held his breath. And as the blanket of intoxication wrapped around his head like a green turban he said, "Where else can you get paid to smoke weed, blow harp and sing the blues?"

"Check it out," said Noodles, the band's keyboard player, as two slender brunettes sauntered across the parking lot on long shapely legs. A pair of tawny lionesses on the prowl, both women wore faded cut-off jeans, coral hued tank tops and a potent dab of pheromone-laced perfume. Their appearance triggered seismic disturbances in the libidinous imagination of every male onboard, causing one girlfriend to jab an elbow into her beau's ribs and say, "What do you think you're looking at, huh, Bucko?"

"I could chew their shorts off and spit out the zippers," said Charlie, as the pair strode across the gangplank.

"Oh yeah? Let's see you do something about it," said Norbert, the band's guitar player. "You're so lame you'd ruin a wet dream."

Before Charlie could respond with an insult of his own, a blast from the Jupiter's air horn made everyone flinch. The distorted sound of the captain's voice followed, on the intercom, buzzing like an angry hornet trapped in an empty Coke bottle. The captain concluded his incomprehensible monolog and pulled the lanyard again, giving everyone another deafening whistle-blast of nautical realism.

At two o'clock the guests were all aboard. The gangplank was withdrawn and the lines cleared. Captain Elmo opened the throttle and the deck shuddered as the barge surged away from the shore, engulfing the passengers at the stern in a choking cloud of diesel fumes. The crowd briefly contemplated all they had left behind on terra firma – their cares, hopes and fears – all except the captain, who downed another shot and envisioned sweat-drenched swabbies below deck, shoveling coal into the red-hot maw of an engine-room furnace.

The Jupiter gathered speed and the sweating crowd welcomed the gentle breeze created by the forward movement. The temperature quickly dropped five degrees, but the humidity didn't budge. And although Old Glory and the Jolly Roger both furled from the antenna mast, no one could say which inspired greater allegiance.

"Battle stations," said Charlie. "Let's open with Tina's favorite song."

Norbert and Waves strapped on their instruments. TR clicked his drumsticks four times to establish tempo and Noodles played the opening organ riff to "96 Tears." The woman behind the bar squealed with delight, rushed out and began to perform a mesmerizing hip swivel reminiscent of a washing machine on the agitate cycle. She danced solo as Norbert chunked chords and Waves played fat bass notes that fought for dominance against the low-frequency throb of the Jupiter's diesel engine.

"You're gonna' cry, cry cry cry, ninety-six tears," warbled Charlie. Then he blew a harmonica solo that sounded like a saxophone in its death throes. The Globster relit his pipe and listened from a breeze-protected nook as the song concluded with an ear-splitting crescendo. Tina blew Charlie a kiss and scurried back to her post behind the bar.

"And there you have it, folks," said Charlie. "The magnificent pageant of life reduced to basics: Intro, two verses, chorus, solo, bridge, last verse, chorus and out."

The party gathered momentum, the boisterous crowd unaware of the immense purple thunderheads rising into the troposphere to the northwest.

* * *

"Batten the hatches!" ordered the Captain as the Jupiter plowed into a squall. Capricious gusts and a sudden downpour whipped the lake's surface into effervescence. The Jupiter's two-man crew lowered Plexiglas shutters, but rainwater trickled through a tiny hole and shorted out Norbert's guitar amp with a loud zapping noise evocative of the electric chair in action.

"Shut it down," Charlie shouted, drawing an index finger laterally across his throat.

The musicians quickly stowed their instruments away, then drew a plastic tarp over the equipment. A sudden enfilade of hailstones clattered onto the deck as the Globster staggered about with a demented smile on his slightly green face. Captain Elmo decided to outflank the squall and spun the wheel, bringing the Jupiter hard about.

The abrupt shift in direction caused the band's PA speakers to topple.

"Look out!" yelled Charlie. Everyone scrambled out of the way and an instant later both heavy speaker cabinets struck the deck with a resounding crash. No one was injured, but at the moment of collapse the Globster had been standing at the stern rail, leaning out and vomiting. When the Jupiter lurched he lost his footing, along with his lunch. Both sneakers slid out from under him and he somersaulted over the side into the water. Not a soul witnessed his abrupt disappearance.

Chapter Thirty-One

The Moira cruised amidst azure haze thick enough to obscure both eastern and western shores and to erase the horizon to the north and south. Squalls formed shifting curtains of rain in the distance. As usual, the holiday brought out hundreds of pleasure craft – sailboats, runabouts and kayaks – all moving in different directions but destined to congregate at Rock Cove around dusk for a front-row seat for the fireworks.

Jade had no difficulty locating Dark Island, in spite of the restricted visibility. Approaching from the north, she cut the engine a hundred yards out from its boulder-strewn edge and waited to see if their arrival would provoke a response from the island's privacy-obsessed overlord.

"We seem to have caught the professor napping," said Roland after ten minutes of radio silence. "Perhaps he's off somewhere, but in any event, now's the time to make an underwater circuit around the island. We may not get the chance again."

"I agree," said Jade. "The computer shows no sign of the moving blotches."

She went below and soon emerged wearing a wetsuit, weight-belt and a sheath knife strapped to one calf. Jade walked to the rear deck, where Roland helped her put on the scuba cylinder and tighten the backpack straps. He opened the regulator's main valve and made sure the reserve lever was in the upright position. Jade took a breath through the mouthpiece and then stepped onto the transom to don a pair of fins, a hood and a mask. She held the mask in place with one hand, made a thumbs up sign with the other and jumped. Her plunge created a swirl of bubbles that quickly dispersed to reveal a green universe filled with countless specks of algae, all suspended like so many tiny galaxies.

Her splash had not gone unnoticed.

The sound radiated outwards through the liquid medium at a speed four times greater than in air. The impulse faded as the distance increased, but not before arousing the curiosity of every lamprey within a large radius.

Propelled by fluid thrusts from her finned feet, Jade swam through water that grew increasingly shallow as she neared the island's flank. She swam around large boulders whose tops protruded above the surface, gliding between angled shafts of sunlight that swept the zebra mussel-encrusted rocks with twisting yellow striations.

Now at a depth of only eight feet, she began an underwater circumnavigation of the island, unaware of the lampreys converging behind the water's translucent curtain, their proximity sensors keening like a horde of living theremins. The gathering swarm bombarded the diver with electrical impulses, but kept their distance, content for the moment to merely stalk this strange being in their midst – an intruder emitting clouds of bubbles and the unfamiliar molecular taste of neoprene.

Jade swam alongside a ledge that intersected the vertical wall of rock to form low cliffs on the island's western flank. She paused at the mouth of a small inlet and surfaced for a look. It was not the inlet that led to Stryker's dock, for its entrance lay concealed by the skeletal branches of the dead cedar still firmly anchored by its roots to the rocks. Curious as to how far it might extend, she submerged and swam between rock walls that gradually shrank in width as she ventured forward.

The lampreys lost their fix on the target. They did not disperse, but hovered and waited.

Jade followed the inlet for approximately 40 feet before encountering a dead-end wall, where the width of the inlet shrank to only 6 feet. She surfaced again and noticed something odd: What had initially appeared to be a natural rock formation now revealed clear signs of artifice – for there, half under the water and half exposed to air, she found a solid metal door set into an aluminum frame. The door bore a thick patina of rust and algae, but its hinges were clean and free of zebra mussels.

Jade realized that the mysterious aperture must still be functional. Why would anyone go to the trouble of installing such a peculiar access, she wondered? And where did it lead? Jade drew her knife and struck the metal surface with its butt – three sharp raps – aware of the absurdity, as if knocking might bring a snorkeling butler along to open it. Not surprising, there was no response. She sheathed the blade, turned and swam back towards the open waters of the lake.

Where the lampreys were waiting.

Jade emerged from the inlet and reentered their probing sensory fields.

The swarm quickly reacquired their target and hunger overcame curiosity. They closed in, coiling and rippling… 20 feet… 15… 10…

Jade turned her head in time to see the leading edge materialize from the undifferentiated wall of green. She whirled around to face her attackers and drew her knife an instant before the swarm enveloped her, wrapping their sinuous lengths around her limbs and pressing their oral hoods onto her wetsuit and fins. She hacked and sliced, but, impeded by the resistance of the water, her movements seemed to occur in slow motion.

Impeded or not, Jade fought with all her strength. Every time she felt the alarming sensation of a lamprey chewing into her wetsuit, she wrenched it away and hewed it in half.

One lamprey pressed its oral hood against the faceplate of her mask. A revolting blade-tipped tongue repeatedly smacked the shatterproof glass until she drove her blade into the creature's flesh. The decapitated lamprey released its suction grip and writhed away in a furious paroxysm of death, adding its share to the expanding cloud of blood staining the water.

Chapter Thirty-Two

The Globster struggled to the surface, sculling frantically with both hands as the Jupiter surged heedlessly away into the squall. A wave dashed him in the face, choking off his cry for help. Rain spattered all around like particles colliding in an atom smasher. Watery lancets stung his eyes and blurred his vision as he wrenched off sneakers now as heavy as cement overshoes. The Jupiter, he realized, was not about to turn around and rescue him. It had been traveling south when he fell overboard, and though difficult to judge, he estimated the distance to the nearest shore to be about a mile. He knew his only hope of survival was to swim.

At 70 degrees, there was no immediate threat of hypothermia, but in an hour the water temperature would not be so forgiving. When he unbuckled his belt to jettison his jeans, the devil-pipe slipped from a pocket and sank into the black depths forever.

Another burst of hail plipped the surface like a million BB's fired from above, ceasing as abruptly as it had begun. A flash of lightning preceded a solitary peal of thunder. The Globster knew a strike in his general vicinity would merely electrocute him, while a close shot would stew the brains in his skull and then burst his eyeballs.

"Think positive, dude," he said aloud.

Something brushed against his leg and the Globster felt a nasty jolt of fear. He knew that an ancient species of gar lived and fed in the lake's gloomy depths – each yard-long fish equipped with a pointed jaw full of long teeth shaped like wicked thorns.

The Globster swam, alternating between the crawl and the breaststroke to conserve energy. He recalled how, as a child, he had watched honeybees and green-eyed horseflies buzzing helplessly in a pool, and how he'd played God – deciding which insects to rescue and which to abandon to fate. As a teenager, he'd been an excellent swimmer; but now, overweight and unused to strenuous exertion, his limbs quickly grew tired and his joints began to hurt.

He swam on, never-the-less, but after ten minutes the shore appeared no closer. The lake had become a merciless foe that would never cease its assault until he stood on solid ground or floated face down, clasped to eternity's cold, wet bosom.

Now, as his ears filled with water – eliminating all sound except the hissing of eardrums listening to themselves – he began to shiver. His head throbbed and the fillings in his teeth ached; the muscles in his shoulders and legs burned with lactic acid and he knew that if he reached the shore he would be sore for a week.

If?

The uncertainty caught him by surprise and the grim thought of failure ricocheted through his head like a Teflon-coated slug. A momentary spike of adrenalin goaded him on, but soon his mind began to wander and spin fantasies: "Tell us about the time you fell overboard and swam across the entire lake," his friends would someday clamor. He imagined how, with each subsequent account of his triumph over Death, the feat would grow – from simple determination to heroic bravery, ultimately attaining the stature of legend.

* * *

Now half a mile away, the Jupiter weathered the squall as easily as a duck caught in a spring shower. When the rain ceased, the crew raised the Plexiglas shutters and swabbed the deck while the band removed the plastic tarp protecting their gear. Although the PA cabinets had suffered damage in the fall, the speakers still functioned. Norbert plugged his guitar into the spare amp he lugged around for just such an emergency. As soon as the PA came back on, Charlie grabbed a microphone and said, "Now hear this! All hands are to eat, drink, dance and have a good time. That is an order."

The passengers raised their beers and cheered.

The party quickly regained its former impetus as the Squirrels played a set of classic rhythm and blues hits. Charlie did his skinny white-boy imitation of a James Brown hit, singing, "I feel good!" During intermission he circulated through the crowd, clapping people on the back and cracking dirty jokes. After fortifying himself with a plate of fried chicken, potato salad, coleslaw and a beer, he introduced himself to the matched pair of brunettes, who, it turned out, were mother and daughter.

"That was some drenching," he said, "but neither of you looks any worse for it. You must be wash and wear women."

"That's right," said Dawn, the elder. "Just hang us on the line and we'll drip dry."

Charlie scrutinized her from behind the safety of his shades. She reminded him of a '56 T-Bird – classic lines and a million miles on the odometer, but plenty of zip under the hood – still able to accelerate from zero to 60 in under three Heinekens.

"Do you have family around here?" he asked.

"All my in-laws are outlaws and all my close friends are far away."

Charlie turned to ogle Sunshine, the younger of the two. The willowy daughter struck him as a miraculous orchid blooming in the manure heap. "If I were a shark," he wanted to say (but didn't), "I'd eat you for breakfast."

Waves pulled up a chair and asked, "Has anyone seen the Globster lately?"

"He's around somewhere," said Charlie. "Probably met someone and they're busy right now learning to tie bowline sheepshanks."

"Why do you call him the Globster?" asked Sunshine.

"His real name is Bob, somewhere along the line Bob became Glob, and then the Globster. He's quite a noble savage – our own little Queequeg – not a cannibal, mind you, although he worships a carved idol he carries with him everywhere he goes."

* * *

At that very moment the subject of their discussion was choking down another mouthful of water. So this is how people drown, the Globster realized. Not all at once, but a little at a time.

He'd been swimming for over 40 minutes and fatigue threatened to overwhelm him. Despair raised its ugly head and stared into his soul. He knew how easy it would be to slip beneath the surface and disappear, once and for all.

Instead, he rolled over to float on his back and gazed at a sky filled not with harmless puffs of summer cumulus, but twisted, wind-whipped wraiths; gaunt visages of the condemned astride skeletal nags with bulging, nightmare eyes.

Tentacles of panic grasped the swimmer as he pondered the awful certainty a convict must face when taking those last shackled steps from death row to the execution chamber painted an innocuous light blue. He shuddered at the thought of entering oblivion on someone else's timetable; to know that – with unassailable certainty – life was about to end and no power on earth or in heaven would intervene.

The swimmer's limbs felt as heavy as the flippers of an elderly, arthritic walrus. And yet, though numb with fatigue, he forced himself to swim, one stroke after another, even though a part of him wanted to lie still, close his eyes and drift away.

After about three minutes, he rolled over, floated on his back and said, "Okay God, it's your call. Give me a sign. Throw me a bone, fer' Chrissakes."

As if at a wizard's command, a beam of sunlight broke through the clouds. Orange radiance reflected from the diaphanous wings of the dragonflies that landed, still copulating, on the island formed by his protuberant stomach.

"Not bad," said the Globster. "I do want a lot more pussy before I die."

Hundreds of silver minnows suddenly plopped and wriggled in the surface waters nearby. Without warning, seagulls swooped down to feast.

"YES!" shouted the Globster, slapping the water and scaring away the gulls.

"Beauty, sex and food!"

Clouds obscured the sun's billion-watt klieg light, although a patch of blue opened elsewhere to reveal a crescent moon slicing along like a dorsal fin.

"I'll tell ya' what, God. If you'll let me reach the shore, I promise to change my ways… I'll quit drinking… I won't get high anymore… Shit, I'll even get a job."

Another fleeting gap in the clouds permitted the heavenly illumination an encore, as if to ratify the Globster's pledge. Fortified with the righteous glow of renewed hope, he rolled over and began a slow but steady stroke towards the western shore.

Imperceptibly, the distance diminished and he could now discern individual trees instead of a featureless gray-green mass. He did not, however, notice the dense mat of floating lake weed that loomed before him. He swam into its tangled fronds and became enmeshed. The more he tried to heave aside the heavy interlocking strands, the more they ensnared. Panic wrestled with his instinct for self-preservation as he snatched a breath, submerged and tried to swim clear of the obstacle.

The ball of his right foot struck a rock, a rock covered with zebra mussels. A razor-sharp shell sliced a deep incision but his growing chill numbed the pain. He submerged once more in hopes of determining the water's depth. Again, his foot touched rock, but gently, inflicting only a shallow cut.

The Globster realized the depth had been decreasing as he drew closer to the shore. After laboriously swimming another hundred feet, he tested the depth again; to his great relief he discovered he could now stand on tiptoe and keep his nose just above the waterline.

The rocky margin beckoned as the Globster struggled forward with aching, leaden limbs. When at last he reached the shallows, he crawled amongst the boulders much like the first proto-amphibian to haul itself onto land hundreds of millions of years ago.

Numb with fatigue and dizzy with exhaustion, he tried to stand but his legs refused to support the weight. He fell, ribs cracking against stone. Dry land waited nearby as he clutched at the slippery stones, dragging himself forward on hands and knees through the shallow water.

An obstacle appeared before him, wedged permanently amongst the coastal rocks – a lost and long-forgotten 18th century tombstone – its inscription effaced by time and the elements. Grateful to be alive, but too stiff and sore to move any further, he leaned his back against its cold, hard surface for a moment's rest.

The Globster stared at the mountains to the east, now bathed in the sun's sanguineous rays. Closing his eyes, he took a deep breath and gathered the last of his strength. A minute later he opened them and watched as numerous snake-like forms undulated towards him through the water. Without a sound, lampreys clamped onto the soles of his feet, sank their teeth into his numbed flesh and injected digestive enzymes. Others slithered near and wrapped themselves around his legs.

The Globster tried to reach down and wrench the disgusting creatures off and smash them against the rocks, but lethargy greater than mere exhaustion crept over him. He hauled his arms up and out of the water and stared with disbelief at the lampreys eating the palms of his hands.

Neurotoxins invaded his bloodstream.

Paralysis overwhelmed him and both arms dropped limply to his sides.

The Globster felt strangely euphoric right up to the instant his brain ignited with searing impulses from every pain receptor in his body. No scream escaped his tingling blue lips, however, only a pitiful whimper.

Respiration grew labored as he slumped against his own tombstone.

And shortly before death gathered him into its capacious fold, he knew the unspeakable torment and irremediable terror of an innocent man facing execution.

Chapter Thirty-Three

Roland sat in the captain's chair, relishing a sense of isolation not unlike that encountered while aloft in a fighter aircraft. I'm a lucky man, he mused, for I have known genuine adventure – and lived to tell about it – not the vicarious, pre-digested alternative provided by the film industry.

He did not consult Jade's laptop and so remained blissfully unaware of his granddaughter's struggle. Instead, he glanced at the LORAN and pondered Columbus's voyage; never in his wildest dreams could the Spaniard have imagined the global grasp of modern technology. Copernicus too would've been flabbergasted by NASA's precise prognostications regarding planetary movement. And what of that old heretic Galileo, he wondered? Would he have been able to comprehend the stunning detail and depth revealed by the Hubble Space Telescope?

Not bloody likely!

The afternoon humidity had grown increasingly oppressive; a purple swath glowered above a horizon, as ominous as the prelude to the Apocalypse. Roland was on the verge of dozing off when he decided to take a refreshing dip. After donning swim trunks, he clambered along the boat's starboard rail and stood atop the forward deck. In another moment or two the venerable rugby player would've jumped over the side, but Jade surfaced nearby and shouted, "Stop! Don't go in the water!"

Roland met her at the stern, hoisted the scuba cylinder up and set it aside while she gripped the swim-ladder, removed one flipper and then the other and tossed them onboard. She climbed out and stood on the transom.

"Your wetsuit is a mess," he said. "What the devil happened?"

"Lampreys attacked me!" she gasped, wrenching off the hood. "Dozens of them."

"You're sure they were lampreys?"

"Yes, damned ugly brutes! I got a good look at the business end when one attached to my faceplate. I killed as many as I could. All of a sudden they dispersed. If I hadn't had a knife, they would've torn me to pieces. I'll never go anywhere ever again without a sharp blade."

Jade stripped off the wetsuit's upper half and held it up. "Look at this," she said, poking a finger through one of the many holes sliced in the half-inch neoprene.

"Did any bite you?"

"No. They tried like hell but I don't think any got their teeth into me."

"Better let me check your back, just to be sure."

"Yes, but what should we do? If we report this to the Coast Guard, they'd probably give us breath and urine tests. We've no proof other than this perforated wetsuit. I should've brought back a specimen. I suppose now I'll have to go back in for one – or for a half – I carved up quite a few."

"Don't push your luck."

"I suppose you're right, but there is one person who knows a thing or two about lampreys and he lives on that damned island. There's something else too; I explored a small inlet that opens on the southwestern edge. The entrance can't be seen from above the surface, but it goes in a long way and leads to a metal door built into the rocks."

"Any idea as to its purpose?"

"Who knows? Another of Stryker's home improvements."

Jade stepped below into the galley, stripped off the lower half of the wetsuit and her bikini, then changed into a pair of khaki shorts and a light pullover.

"I need a drink," she called out. "Care for one?"

"Spot on."

Roland and his granddaughter settled onto the boat's padded Naugahyde couch, gin and tonics in hand. "It's so tranquil I find it difficult to imagine you fighting for your life only minutes ago."

Jade sat bolt upright. "We've forgotten to check the computer!"

Before she could get to her feet, the Moira tilted abruptly, then righted.

"What was that?" she asked. "Did a wake just hit us?"

Her grandfather looked over the side and said, "Hell's bloody bells!"

Roland and Jade stared at a vast number of lampreys floating languidly at the surface, surrounding the boat for a radius of 30 feet, each serpentine back covered with mottled brown patterns.

The lampreys stared back through a multitude of shiny, black eyes, each orb no larger than a BB. The swarm silently appraised the two humans perched nearby, then, in unison, the creatures began to undulate, fanning the water with their bodies.

"I had no idea they gathered in such large concentrations," said Jade.

"They're not supposed to."

A minute later the entire swarm submerged. A multitude of sucker disks fastened onto the hull, each a living suction cup filled with orange teeth.

An awful screech filled the air as they began to gouge and notch the Fiberglas; a far more distressing sound than fingernails raked across a blackboard or the crunch of sand in a sandwich.

"They're gnawing the hull!" said Roland. "I suggest we leave, immediately!"

Jade leapt to the controls and started the engine. She engaged the transmission and opened the throttle, but steering was difficult and the boat responded sluggishly due to the combined mass and weight of the attached swarm. Jade opened up the big V-8 and spun the wheel back and forth, hoping to dislodge them, but they held fast. Nor could the roar of the engine drown out the dreadful noise of plastic being notched and rent by countless chiseling teeth.

SQREEECK!

"They're awfully determined," said Roland.

"Determined to do what?"

"Sink us and eat us, I suspect."

The lampreys gnawed deeper and the chiseling noise grew louder, amplified by the boat's hollow interior. The swarm penetrated the Fiberglas. Only the tenuous seal created by their oral hoods prevented an immediate inrush of water. They released their grip and it was then that Roland and Jade heard the worst sound a mariner can know – the steady whoosh of water sluicing in through the hull.

"We're breached!" Jade shouted. "Take the wheel while I see if I can plug it."

The galley was already awash as she descended, splashing through a foot of water, flinging open storage cabinet doors in search of the rupture.

"We're sinking! There's no way I can stop it," she yelled as the water rose to her knees. "It's coming in behind a locker where I can't get to it!"

"I'll aim for those boulders," Roland replied. "Maybe I can berth us in their midst."

Lake water flooded in and killed the engine, but momentum carried them forward. More terrible sounds filled their ears as the Moira went down – the hull scraping against stone as it settled at a 30-degree angle on the bottom – bow pointed up, high and dry above the surface.

Suddenly the hull gave way and a torrent of lamprey-infested water poured in. Jade threw herself onto the padded sleeping platform beneath the foredeck, then turned to watch the coiling mass fill the cabin – hundreds of sinuous bodies threshing the bedding, clothes and pillows into twisted, sodden bundles. Jade looked up through the open hatch and marveled for an instant at how serene the little square of sky looked. But when the water reached the platform she grasped the sides of the hatch and pulled herself up and through, extracting her legs an instant before the swarm engulfed the berth.

"Thank God you're all right," said Roland, kneeling on the bow alongside her.

The Moira trembled as the lampreys lashed the cabin in a fit of primal fury, hurling debris around the flooded interior like an enormous food processor set to puree. The frenzy continued as they pried open every cabinet door, flogging their bodies like living whips, churning everything into chaos.

A minute later the terrible noise subsided. Having found nothing edible, the swarm dispersed and returned to the lake.

"I think they're gone," said Roland.

"Yes, but we're stranded."

Although the perimeter of Dark Island was no more than 40 feet away, neither Roland nor Jade felt inclined to swim the short distance. Instead, they sat on the bowsprit with their backs against the rail and watched the clouds congealing in the western sky.

Jade heaved a sigh, then pushed the deck hatch with her foot, slamming it shut.

Chapter Thirty-Four

The party onboard the Jupiter intensified, along with the humidity, even though it didn't seem possible for the atmosphere to hold another molecule of moisture without triggering a monsoon.

The afternoon heat diminished only slightly as evening encroached on the day.

All thoughts of the Globster had long since vanished as the Jupiter cruised across the broad lake and into the diminutive bay at Rock Cove. Once alongside the dock, the Squirrels transferred their equipment to a wooden stage situated before a wide sloping lawn already filled with spectators. Nearby, the fireworks technicians finalized their preparations.

Sergeant Edwards was busy on the other side of the resort, waving his arms in a valiant attempt to direct the ceaseless flow of incoming traffic. The field designated for parking was jammed; the overflow threatened to inundate the grass airstrip. The officer would've preferred to rove freely, but a record number of visitors had descended upon the resort, overwhelming the little troop of beleaguered rent-a-cops, thereby preventing him.

Weeks before, Elsbeth had spoken to Charlie about hiring the band, specifically instructing him not to begin their show until after the orchestra's performance. But with no sign of an orchestra, the leader of the Squirrels paced back and forth across the stage impatiently.

"Those 'shrooms I ate are sure coming on fast," said Charlie, grinning from ear to ear as the alkaloids percolated within the bony glockenspiel he called a head. To celebrate the national holiday, he'd booked a flight on Trans-Love Airways – a psilocybin-fueled trip with a seat by the window, Hunter S. Thompson at the stick and God as his copilot.

Unable to wait any longer, Charlie turned to the band and asked, "Are we ready to rock?"

"Good to go, mon," said TR, seated behind the drums.

"My board is green," said Noodles.

"Launch it," said Norbert.

"Who's the biggest, baddest frog in the pond?" asked Waves, eager to belt out low-frequency notes on his Fender bass.

A moment before TR counted down the first tune, a trio of F-16's hurtled by – three silver needles flying extremely low in tight formation. The noise was sudden, violent and deafening.

"Nothing like an ostentatious rattle of the sword to keep the locals in line," said Waves.

Charlie selected a harmonica in the correct key as the band kicked off with an old Chicago blues number, a tune about mojos and black cat bones. But halfway through . . . WHUMP! The launch of the first rocket caught everyone by surprise as it ascended into a sky not yet sufficiently dark.

BOOM!

A crimson starburst marked its apogee. A split-second later the shockwave hit like a boxer's right hook, followed by cheers and a shower of glowing cinders that rained down on the stage and burned a wisp of hair in the middle of Charlie's incipient bald spot.

"What the flux?" he barked. "Do they really expect us to play alongside Mount Vesuvius while it's erupting?" Suddenly a rocket exploded prematurely on the launch pad. Sparking bits of blue and gold went zinging by like tracers. "Ha! Ya' missed," Charlie crowed, capering like a Merry Prankster, his sugar-glazed vision pulsing with psychedelic colors and flickering afterimages derived from an excess of neurotransmitters.

The Winooski Winds had reassembled outside the resort's dining hall and now the bombastic sound of Souza marches competed with the amplified sizzle and thud produced by the Squirrels.

* * *

The lurid, particulate-laden rays of the setting sun bathed the Moira in honey-colored light, and the air relinquished the last vestige of movement. A candle's flame would not have wavered a millimeter as Roland and Jade perched atop the Moira's angled bow.

"I feel as if I've been shot down over enemy territory," said Roland. "The radio is dead, the depth finder is superfluous and the LORAN is a preposterous joke. Not only that, but your laptop is ruined . . . Have I forgotten anything?"

"No, but at least we know exactly where we are," Jade replied. "The island's so close I'm tempted to swim for it."

"Highly inadvisable. The lampreys are still out there."

"Do you think we'll be stranded for long?"

"I expect the RAF will be dispatching a rescue chopper any minute. Actually, we could be here a while. Someone's bound to spot us, though. Our best bet is to sit tight and wait."

"We may not have found Champ, but if what you said about the lamprey swarm being an aberration is true, it's a sensational discovery. If not, how could they have accumulated in such numbers without anyone knowing?"

"Good question, but don't forget – parts of this lake are 400 feet deep; who knows what may be lurking in the deepest trenches?"

As evening faded into twilight and night unfurled its purple cloak from the east, the stranded mariners heard the incessant quavering whine of a million midges swerving through the air – an entire insect aerodrome hovering erratically in shifting clouds – a bug buffet for the bats that veered about, their sonar set to full auto.

On the far northwestern shore the lights of Westport shone as constant as stars. Only five miles away, they might as well have been the Pleiades.

"Somewhere below there must be a flare-pistol," said Roland. "Every boat this size is required by law to have one. If we found it we could summon help."

"I'll take a look," said Jade.

"It would be in a plastic case the size of a small toolbox."

Jade raised the forward hatch and peered into the boat's dim, flooded interior. Bits of debris floated motionlessly atop a waterline that bisected the cabin at an angled plane parallel to the lake's surface. "It looks empty," she said. "I'm going in."

"Be as quick and quiet as you can."

She gripped the sides of the hatch and lowered her legs, insinuating her way into the cool water up to her waist. Items that had escaped destruction floated here and there, a plastic jar filled with peanuts, a waterproof flashlight. She tucked them both under one arm and then reached below the water to pluck the retaining pin from the refrigerator's door. She extracted two bottles – one of gin, the other tonic. Jade made her way back to the bow and thrust all but the flashlight into Roland's hands. Then she turned, switched on the flashlight and submerged, reappearing fifteen seconds later with a red plastic box. She handed the box and the light to Roland, who set them aside before taking hold of her hand and hoisting her up and through the hatch.

"Well done," he said. "I only wish I had a towel to offer you."

"I'll settle for a snack and a stiff drink."

Roland pointed the flashlight down into the flooded cabin. The beam penetrated into the water and cast an eerie green aura. Movement beneath the surface caught his eye as one lamprey after another swam through the tinted liquid in search of the cause of the recent disturbance. Within moments the cabin contained dozens of hungry predators. "Bloody hell," he said. "Just look at that. If the boat can fill so quickly with the little buggers, there must be plenty in the vicinity."

He lowered the hatch as Jade uncapped the bottles and took a swig from each.

"Let's see what we have," he said, opening the plastic case to reveal a flare gun and three cartridges the size of shotgun shells, each designed to produce a six-second burn. After inserting a cartridge, he cocked the hammer and pointed the gun aloft. But before he could fire he saw a burst of color low in the northern sky – a bright red sphere that expanded briefly before winking out, followed by a distant boom that took twelve seconds to cover the distance and reach their ears.

"Fireworks?"

"The resort's Independence Day celebration must be starting," said Jade.

"I'd forgotten about the American holiday; I'm accustomed to seeing fireworks on Guy Fawke's Day. But that's good, it means there's a damned good chance any number of boats will pass by afterward. I think I'll hold off on the flare till then."

Roland put the flare pistol back in its case, picked up the flashlight and aimed it at the lake, sweeping the beam in a 360-degree rotation. Hundreds of tiny eyes glistened with reflected light as the swarm floated quietly at the surface once again. "Christ! We could sit here all night while they wait for us like the croc that ate Captain Hook's hand."

"Could we frighten them off with a flare?"

"I doubt it would have much effect, but the anchor might if I were to swing it like a truncheon. Maybe if I crushed a few it would drive them off. I'm going to give it a go."

Roland unlocked the davit and lifted the steel anchor from its cradle on the bowsprit. He stood with feet apart and began to swing it back and forth, gradually letting out more rope as the width of the pendulum's sweep increased. At the point where the arc became a loop, he flung the anchor down, into the swarm. It struck and produced a splash, but little else. "I'm going to try again," he said, pulling in the line. But before he could, the swarm silently submerged.

Chapter Thirty-Five

Twilight seemed to linger longer than usual as the crowd sat waiting for the fireworks to begin. The crepuscular hour arrived, followed closely by the leading edge of a storm system roiling with electrical energy. It approached from the west – still many miles beyond the Adirondacks – faint pulses of lightning glimmering a little brighter with every passing minute.

The Ticonderoga arrived late; the ship churning along with only its red and green navigation lights on. Captain Griffis waited until he was a half-mile from the cove before hitting a switch. Instantly, hundreds of tiny white bulbs strung from every cornice and rail lit up and the vessel appeared to materialize out of thin air. Hearty cheers greeted its dramatic arrival. The Ti's captain responded with a blast from a steam whistle, then reversed engines and brought the ship to a graceful halt in the center of the cove.

WHUMP!

Another rocket went up. This one scattered hundreds of small firecrackers that exploded with a sound like the crackle of tumultuous applause.

The members of the Green Mountain Philharmonic watched attentively as Guillermo von Hesse, the maestro, tapped his baton and raised his arms to signal the imminent downbeat to the first movement of Beethoven's Pastoral Symphony.

The strings wove a graceful introduction, an alternatively thoughtful and jubilant motif. The sound carried well in the humid air. Thousands of music lovers heard the combined output of the Green Mountain Philharmonic, the Winooski Winds and Squirrels in the Attic – an appalling blend that filled the sultry air with Beethoven, Souza and Howlin' Wolf – a discordant mix that only Charles Ives could appreciate (the world premier of the "Squirrel Symphony," perhaps, or a deviant avant-garde composition entitled "Philip and Ludwig in the Attic").

Not to be outdone, the fireworks technicians began to light fuses, but at a leisurely pace. Each projectile tumbled end over end, high into the sable darkness, detonating with a vision-blurring explosion, followed by a drizzle of glowing embers that drifted down to scorch tiny holes in the orchestra's sheet music.

Countless mosquitoes descended upon the crowd and all three musical ensembles, striking with a frenzy last seen by Japanese pilots attacking Pearl Harbor. The musicians had no choice but to ignore the rocket's red glare, the bombs bursting in midair, and the murderous, bloodthirsty insects.

When Beethoven's symphonic thunderstorm struck, the orchestra sweated like stevedores. The violinists skittered up and down ebony fingerboards on slender, tapered fingers; the bassists gripped their bows and sawed their way through two pages of zigzagging sixteenth notes intended to denote lightning. Percussionists hammered tympani while the piccolo player emitted an estrogen-charged squeal that modulated up a half step. The Squirrels were loud enough to compete with the orchestra, but not loud enough to prevail against the firework's deafening explosions directly above.

The fireworks crew set off a ground display. A dazzling curtain of silver sparks erupted into the air and burned brightly for half a minute, leaving behind an impenetrable screen of acrid, white smoke. The cloud remained intact as it drifted ever so slowly towards the stage. Lit from within by flares, the launch crew leapt through the crimson fog like Beelzebub's roadies.

Waves saw the cloud drifting closer and yelled, "It's toxic! Don't breathe it!"

A moment later he unplugged his bass, jumped off the stage and escaped into the intermittent darkness. One inhalation was enough to convince the remaining Squirrels to follow suit and the song ended with what is known in rock 'n roll parlance as a train wreck.

Undaunted by the shuddering explosions or the sporadic brilliance from above, maestro von Hesse staggered about the podium, slicing the air with his baton, perspiration pouring from his brow.

Captain Griffis stood on the upper deck of the Ticonderoga, watching the storm's approach from the west. He congratulated himself on having parked the old girl in the cove, the most sheltered berth a mariner could hope for.

Ludwig's thunderstorm lapsed into quiescence as the real one loomed ever closer. A spasm of giddy apprehension rippled through the crowd as a blinding flash of electricity illuminated the entire sky. A simultaneous clap of thunder drowned out the puny squibs still being flung up from below.

The first violinist noticed something odd: Each time she tapped her foot on the deck it produced a small but unequivocal splash. She stopped playing and peered down. Von Hesse glared at her, but other musicians became aware of the liquid at their feet and mutiny swept the ranks of the classically trained. The Sixth Symphony wheezed to an unscheduled and undignified conclusion.

The explosions and the mounting thunder prevented Captain Griffis from hearing the shouts or the rush of feet across the lower deck and up the stairs. Leading the charge, still clutching her instrument, the first violinist ran up to him and yelled, "WE'RE SINKING!"

"Calm yourself," he replied. "We couldn't be any safer than here in this sheltered cove."

A purple burst illuminated the woman's wet footprints across the deck. The captain took one look, then strode onto the bridge and stared with disbelief at the alarm lights blinking on the console.

"This can't be happening," he muttered, hastening to the rail for a look over the side. Indeed, the vessel rode extremely low in the water and the main deck was already awash with several inches. Dashing back to the bridge, he snatched the microphone to alert the Coast Guard, but before he could say "mayday," the electrical system shorted out and the Ticonderoga went black.

Maestro von Hesse stood in the dark and watched, speechless, as his minions deserted their posts and clambered towards the stairs, pushing and shoving and splashing with every step.

The fireworks technicians nervously decided it was high time for the grand finale. They touched off the remaining fuses with their flares...

WHUMP! WHUMP! WHUMP! WHUMP! WHUMP! WHUMP! WHUMP!

Rocket after rocket hurtled aloft in an all-out retaliatory strike that dazzled the eye, assaulted the ear and hammered the solar plexus. For 60 seconds the sky above the cove resembled the Big Bang itself, a blinding onslaught of brilliant colors and concussive detonations.

Finally, when everyone thought it would never end... it did.

The silence exposed the rumble of man-made shock waves receding into the distance, a sound reminiscent of a bowling tournament conducted on a countywide alley.

Abrupt winds whipped up clouds of dust. The crowd began to rouse itself as blinding purple radiance turned night into day for a split second. The rising gale shredded the cordite smoke nebulas drifting above the cove like ghosts exceeding their expiration date. Thunderous hammer-blows cleaved the heavens as the sluice gates opened; torrential rain instantly soaked thousands of spectators as they rushed away in a mad stampede, trampling every one of Elsbeth's cherished perennial flowers.

The frantic exodus quickly overwhelmed the resort's aging security guards. Sergeant Edwards strode once more into the automotive gridlock with a flashlight in each hand and rainwater coursing from the brim of his hat. A welter of cars broke ranks and veered across the landing strip, gouging deep ruts before bogging down, rear wheels spinning futilely.

The deluge shorted out the Squirrel's amps, which, being connected to shore power, blew the circuit breakers and cast the entire resort into darkness!

Bedlam erupted in the dining room as indignant guests shouted demands, while waiters bearing food-laden trays collided and expensive gourmet dinners crashed to the floor. Elsbeth fought to impose order, but her stream of hysterical commands went unheeded and her jurisdiction squirted away faster than a greased pig at the county fair. She wanted to scream with sheer frustration, but instead, gave up and sank wearily onto a couch in the main lobby.

All drinks were now unofficially "on the house," thus precipitating a bout of over-indulgence among guests and staff alike – an impromptu bacchanal in which all class boundaries vanished along with the electricity.

Snee waltzed into the lobby holding an open bottle of Dom Perignon in each hand, the bubbly recently pilfered from a table in the dining room. He noticed Elsbeth sitting despondently in the dim glow cast by a battery-powered emergency light. The artist smiled broadly, presented her with a bottle of Dom and said, "The best-laid men have mice and plans!"

Chapter Thirty-Six

Fitful gusts drove across the lake as Roland and Jade sat on the Moira's angled bow eating peanuts and sipping gin. The booze and salty snack did little to divert their minds from the problem of being marooned, and the growing discomfort caused by sitting on a hard, angled surface with only a narrow railing to lean against.

"We're in for it now," said Roland as the first spatters of rain struck and the sky above the Adirondacks flickered from jet black to vivid amethyst. The fireworks were too far away to appear more than dots of color, blooming for just an instant before disappearing. Suddenly a vast electrical pulse illuminated the interior of the clouds overhead – an orange and purple spasm reminiscent of a nighttime nuclear blast at Yucca Flats – followed by a stupendous rip of thunder.

Without warning the lampreys formed a moving column, a living battering ram that swept in over the sunken stern and plunged into the flooded cabin. The swarm angled up and burst through the forward deck hatch, bashing it off its hinges. Momentum and gravity carried most of the lampreys over the side, but some landed on the narrow bow and began to wriggle towards the stranded mariners.

Roland snapped the flashlight on and then used it to bludgeon the advancing creatures. Jade kicked at them but quickly retracted her feet at the sight of a lamprey considerably larger than its brethren – a glistening monstrosity only inches away, its repulsive oral hood gaping wide, dozens of spiky teeth gnawing the air.

Jade grabbed the pistol and fired a flare into its ugly gullet.

The lamprey contorted violently and dropped over the side.

"Good shot," Roland shouted above the roar of the wind.

"Do you think I killed it?"

"Either that or you gave it a bad case of heartburn. But at least it's gone."

"They behaved as if they'd agreed upon a plan. How could they do that?"

"Yes, it did resemble some rudimentary form of group behavior. They're not supposed to be able to do that either."

"Look there," said Jade, pointing to the red light on the bow of a speedboat as it attempted to outflank the storm. She reloaded and cocked the flair-gun.

"Don't fire yet," Roland cautioned. "Wait till it gets closer."

Thirty seconds later, when the speedboat was a thousand feet away and as close as it would ever be, she raised the gun and pulled the trigger.

Nothing.

She tried again but heard only the snap of the hammer.

"A dud!" she hollered, ejecting the cartridge and inserting the last one. Once again she held the gun up and pulled the trigger. But this time they heard a gratifying bang and watched as the flare etched a brilliant comet across a tormented sky.

The couple in the speedboat turned their attention from the storm to watch the flare's bright arc. "I've always loved Roman candles," said the woman.

"No honey," said the man. "Roman candles shoot fireballs. That's a skyrocket."

The speedboat continued its dash.

"Get your finger out, man!" Roland shouted when he realized the speedboat was not about to stop and offer assistance. "There's a lesson to remember," he exclaimed. "Never fire a distress flare in America on the Fourth of July and expect help."

"Idiots!" said Jade. "But what does his finger have to do with it?"

"Oh, I suppose you're old enough now to know. That's just a bit of very old British slang concerning foreplay."

Before either could say another word the gale struck like an invisible freight train. Bullets of rainwater flew horizontally, striking and stinging every inch of exposed skin. Exposed to the storm's wrath, they had no choice but to turn their backs to the rain, cling to the railing and huddle, heads down and knees drawn up, silently enduring all the sky could hurl at them.

* * *

Charlie stood on the empty stage, soaked to the bone, peaking on mushrooms and laughing like a maniac as the wind clawed at his hair and the rain spat in his eye. Waves and the other Squirrels had departed after hurriedly dismantling their drenched equipment. The Winooski Winds had also dispersed, but onboard the Ticonderoga, the musicians unable to climb the stairs and squeeze onto the upper deck found themselves standing in rising water now up to their shins.

Many of the smaller instruments – the strings and woodwinds – had been passed from hand to hand to the shelter of the upper deck, but the larger ones – the basses and percussion – had been abandoned.

"I'm going to swim ashore," said one of the trombonists when the water reached crotch height. "Why not? I'm already drenched and it can't be more than a hundred feet."

The idea spread rapidly amongst the other musicians on the lower deck.

Captain Griffis was among the symphonic refugees stuck on the upper deck. He was unable to see the water rising up the stairs, but he heard and felt the dreadful grating shudder of the hull as it settled on the cove's rocky bottom.

With the water now waist-high, the tuba, trombone, French horn and bass players climbed over the railing and plunged in for a lightning-lashed dip. Impeded by the weight of wet clothing, they kicked off shoes, trousers and tuxedo jackets, then flung away their bowties. They swam but they did not swim alone.

Thousands of lampreys ranging in size from 18 to 26 inches entered the cove. They circled the Ticonderoga's hull, quivering with excitement, their sensory fields overlapping and crackling like radios all transmitting on the same frequency. The swarm detected the humans splashing above, their clumsy efforts scenting the water with the molecular taste of sweat and flesh.

Viewed from below, each pulse of lightning silhouetted the swimmers against the agitated surface. Instinct and hunger asserted their primordial demands and the lampreys veered away from their communal orbit, individual entities once more, intent upon slaking a ravenous appetite.

The attack was so rapid and unexpected the musicians scarcely knew what hit them. Bewilderment quickly yielded to fear and then to panic as a multitude of squirming predators surged amongst them, coiling and biting. Naked arms and legs offered no resistance to the puncturing teeth or to sharp bony tongues hacking into muscle and sinew. Potent digestive enzymes coursed through the musician's bloodstreams. Moments later their struggles ceased. They vanished beneath the surface, where a feeding frenzy quickly reduced their bodies to gnawed skeletons.

But even so, nine humans could not supply sufficient nutrition for so many hungry carnivores. The lucky few feasted while the majority tasted only frustration. Once the available meat had been consumed the lampreys turned upon one another – the larger snatching and eating the smaller – the intense underwater darkness punctuated by purple light stained green with algae and red with blood.

* * *

Charlie watched from the water's edge and grew puzzled when lightning revealed the swimmers bobbing like corks one minute, but only empty water the next. Perhaps they were hidden by the cattails growing along the cove's edge, he thought. And so, seized by a rare altruistic impulse, he waded in to lend a helping hand.

A lamprey encircled an ankle.

Charlie reached down to yank it away, thinking he'd been snagged by lake weed. Instead, he gripped the wriggling horror and held it up before his dilated eyes. A flash of lightning revealed his mistake. He recoiled and dropped the revolting creature as others darted forward to attack. They clamped onto his legs and he staggered and fell, scrabbling through the mud as more lampreys attached and bit through his clothes. Charlie screamed and thrashed as they bit into his stomach and swallowed alkaloid-enriched blood, but the onset of paralysis was rapid and his struggles ceased.

Charlie's expanded consciousness slowly faded as the lampreys went about their grizzly task. Death was slow in claiming him, however, and he endured an eternity of transcendent pain unrivaled since Torquemada's fiendish reign as inquisitor general during the Spanish Inquisition.

The lampreys fed until all that remained was a bearded, longhaired skull, an earring, ligaments clinging to bones, shredded fabric, a zipper, a pair of sneakers and a blues harp in the key of D.

* * *

Although the resort was in a shambles, Snee was delighted with the day's turn of events: He'd eaten well – his pockets bulged with morsels nicked from the buffet – and he still clutched half a bottle of expensive champagne. The music and the fireworks had been amusing, but the storm was proving to be even more entertaining.

Heedless of the wind and pelting rain, he wandered outside to stare at the forked electricity flickering amongst the clouds like a snake's tongue. Snee shook his fist at the sky and hollered, "Blow ye winds and crack! Do your utmost, blast me as I stand!"

The heavens complied with a blinding ignition and a thunderclap that sounded like Charles Atlas tearing in half every Manhattan phone book ever printed. Millions of volts struck a nearby beech tree and scorched a groove the length of its trunk. Damp soil and tree roots conveyed the voltage outward, charging Snee through wet sneakers. The jolt was not strong enough to kill him, but substantial enough to evoke an impromptu sailor's hornpipe. The threadbare artist danced spasmodically as a blue wreath of St. Elmo's fire encircled his head. Convinced his moment of cosmic retribution had come at last, Snee fell onto all fours, raised his head and howled!

Howard Burdock had lingered behind after the crowd fled, sheltering on the porch attached to the dining hall. He spotted Snee baying like a hound and rushed to his aid, Howard grasped him under the armpits and hauled him to his feet, then rushed him across the lawn, through the ruined flowerbeds and on towards the parking field, where Marion Witherspoon sat waiting for the chaotic traffic jam to subside. She took one look, rolled down her window and said, "He looks like a drowned rat, Howard. Put him in the backseat. He can stay in my guest cottage tonight."

* * *

The rain slackened and stopped. The lightning grew sporadic and the thunder faded as the storm moved off to the east. A profound change came over the swarm once the smaller lampreys in their midst had been eliminated. All further aggression ceased, as did bioelectric scanning. Instead, thousands of lampreys mingled unseen in the dark water, their bodies swaying in rhythmic undulations, hovering in response to a command implanted deep in their genetic structure – the irresistible compulsion to reproduce.

The time to hunt and feed had ended.

The time to spawn grew near.

By dawn, the lampreys in the cove would all be dead.

Chapter Thirty-Seven

At midnight the wind had abated but the lake's surface still churned with restless energy. The temperature had fallen 20 degrees. The humidity was gone, swept away by incoming high pressure to reveal the Milky Way glittering with bright, chilly indifference.

"Ahoy there!"

The hail snapped Roland back from the memory of a cold, dreary November day long ago – a cheerless foggy afternoon punctuated by the sound of mud-spattered athletes battering one another on a rugby pitch in the north of England. Jade was also far away, replaying the memory of a sun-splashed sail in the Caribbean.

A rowboat approached through the darkness; a spotlight illuminated the two figures huddled on the tip of the Moira's bow. "Not a good night to be out on the lake," said Dr. Stanley Stryker.

Roland looked up and said, "Yes, we seem to have pranged our yacht."

"I'll move in closer so you can climb aboard."

Jade lowered herself into the rowboat first and sat at the bow, still holding the flashlight and a bottle containing a mix of gin and tonic. Roland's bare feet were cold and his joints were stiff from inactivity, so it took him a minute to maneuver across the sloping deck on hands and knees before joining her in the rowboat.

"I observed your flare from the mainland," said Stryker, plying the oars. "I returned late from the university and had to wait for the storm to pass and the turbulence to subside before venturing across. How did you end up in such a sorry state?"

"A bloody great swarm of lampreys attacked and sank us."

"What a splendid imagination you have!"

"It's true," said Jade. "They chewed through the hull and scuttled the boat."

"That's ridiculous," said Stryker. "What proof can you offer?"

"Proof? Take a look at the boat," Roland replied. "Do you think I made those holes with my Swiss Army knife?" He paused to regain his composure and then continued in a lower tone of voice.

"Now you listen to me, Stanley. The water around this little island of yours is teeming with lampreys. How do you explain that? And what is the purpose of your secret underwater channel?"

Stryker stopped rowing – the slap of the surface-chop the only sound. "Well, well, well," he said at last. "You've been awfully busy little beavers, haven't you? Prying into the lake's secrets – my secrets – sticking your noses into matters that don't concern you. And then, you're shocked when something comes along and tries to bite it off."

"Take us ashore immediately," said Roland, "or I'll – "

"Or you'll what?" interrupted the professor, revealing a silver-plated Italian 25-caliber pistol. "You will do as I say or I will put a small hole in your favorite liver."

The old pilot heaved a sigh of resignation. Not only had he been shot down over enemy lines, but captured as well. "So be it," he said, "but I demand an explanation."

"You are in no position to demand anything. However, I do intend to provide a demonstration. Rest assured, a most edifying seminar awaits you both."

Stryker resumed rowing after first placing the pistol in his jacket pocket where he could grab it quickly, if necessary. The rowboat moved steadily through the cool night air; the surface-action diminished as they entered the inlet leading to the dock. Once alongside it, Stryker climbed out and secured the rowboat with a chain and a padlock. He took the little gun out of his pocket and pointed it at his captives and then, with a lateral flick of the wrist, ordered them out and onto the path. Jade went first, scything the ground with her flashlight; Roland followed, the island's sovereign trailing.

Their progress ended 50 feet on when Jade encountered an ancient cedar tree that had toppled during the storm, pushed over by a powerful straight-line gust to create a massive obstacle that could not be easily outflanked in the darkness.

"Keep going," Stryker ordered. "Climb through it."

Jade picked her way amongst the tangled branches and over the slippery trunk. She paused to gaze up at the constellation Cygnus – the swan – now clearly visible in the newly created gap in the canopy. Roland followed, moving carefully between the wet fronds. He grasped the narrow end of a stout branch and held on as he passed, flexing it back like an English longbow. Roland waited until the right moment before letting go. The bough whipped back, clouted the professor squarely in the face and knocked him sprawling amidst the branches.

Jade took advantage of the momentary distraction, doused her light and melted into the night as swiftly as a green-eyed puma. Stryker snapped off a shot but hit only air.

"She won't get far," he muttered, regaining his footing and dabbing the blood from his bruised cheek with a handkerchief. "Now, get going!"

The two men extricated themselves from the branches and followed the path till it opened into the clearing. Stryker swept his torch across a scene that had become all but unrecognizable: A freak hundred-miles-an-hour gust had devastated the forest. Many of the largest trees had snapped in half and fallen onto Stryker's fortress, crumpling the roof, shattering every mirrored window and carpeting the ground with a million jagged shards. A tree had fallen on the other side of the building, crushing the shed that housed a propane tank the size of the fabled Fat Man of Los Alamos. Gas hissed quietly from its damaged regulator.

Stryker walked across the mosaic of shattered glass, opened the door to the ground floor and switched on the fluorescent tubes. Undamaged aquariums still lined the walls as he strode past and into the lab, where the steady hum of circulating pumps reassured him that all three holding-tanks remained undisturbed. The professor skirted the tanks and walked to the edge of the lab's most singular feature – a pool built into the concrete floor, measuring 20-feet per side and 6-feet deep.

A faint sound made the professor spin around.

Roland stood in the doorway.

Torn between the desire to eliminate all interference and the need to share the results of his work with someone capable of understanding, Stryker pocketed the little gun and said, "Consider yourself on academic probation. You may enter."

Roland peered into the nearest of three large holding tanks. The trough stood waist high and contained countless young eels, all swimming with just enough force to maintain their positions against the artificial current.

"You, too, have been busy," said Roland. "Are these the local variety?"

"No, Petromyzon Marinus are in that second enclosure. Those are Asian swamp eels. As I mentioned during your previous visit, they are miracles of adaptive evolution, making them ideal for my work. Unlike the lamprey – which has only one or two tricks up its sleeve – swamp eels are the virtuosi of survival."

"A trait we seem to share," said Roland.

"Indeed. But, as vegetarians, they were disinclined towards predation."

"What do you mean by that?"

Stryker smiled and continued, "Through hard work and the wonder of science, I've rectified that unfortunate omission in their behavioral repertoire. The third holding tank contains a genetic hybrid, a creature recently endowed with only the most useful characteristics possessed by the lamprey and the Asian swamp eel."

"What about the swarm that sank our boat? Was that a 'miracle of adaptive evolution' too?"

"The ability to sink a boat came as a complete surprise to me."

"So, it wasn't the result of your, shall we say… intervention?"

"Mother Nature, in her infinite wisdom, seems to have eclipsed my efforts with a timely mutation of her own; in which case, I couldn't be more delighted."

"What about the recent unexplained deaths? They all appear to be the result of predation. Are you responsible? Aren't there enough predators out there already?"

"Far from it. Humans have been blithely eliminating every predatory species extant in a world fast running out of them. Consider the tigers, the wolves, even rattlesnakes – all about to be wiped out by man's stupidity and greed. The rate of species extinction has increased drastically in recent years. Sadly, this loss has not been counteracted by the addition of anything new. And so, to fill this widening gap, I've created a slippery little monster that will proliferate far and wide – as ubiquitous as the mosquito – a silent, voracious hunter that will prey upon the one species that threatens the entire planet . . . Mankind!"

"Is it immortality you seek, or revenge?"

"Either will do. You of all people should know better than to ask. Who else has devoted his life to searching for the beastie?"

"My work will not inflict a menace upon the world. Perhaps you are the monster."

"Really? What a singular notion."

"Why not devote your considerable talent and energy to combating the threat to endangered species; why not replenish those species most at risk?"

"I considered that option, but my approach will be far more gratifying. I intend to release healthy breeding specimens into every body of fresh water I can find, from here to the west coast. My genetically altered progeny will propagate with glorious abandon; their range will expand via the inland waterway; they'll thrive in the Great Lakes. And by the time anyone realizes what's happening, it'll be too late!"

"Your actions will have unforeseen consequences for you and for humanity. Must you feed your ego in this way?"

"Ah yes, humanity," mused Stryker. "I don't give a flying fandango about unforeseen consequences and I've no need to feed my ego, although there will be a great deal of feeding, nevertheless."

"Earlier, you mentioned a demonstration."

"Indeed, and you shall have it. After years of work and countless failures, I succeeded in mastering the technique of gene splicing; to say nothing of the process whereby mutations are selectively induced."

"During the attack that sank our boat, Jade and I witnessed what could only be described as cooperative behavior among the lampreys. How did you accomplish that?"

"One of my greatest achievements," said Stryker. "First, I found it necessary to understand the mechanism controlling cooperation amongst members of various species, the precise language of electrochemical communication prevalent in insects, sponges and a host of other, far more humble creatures. Consider the slime mold: This single-celled organism spends most of its life doing little except to eat. Then, at the release of a highly specific chemical signal, millions upon millions of cells begin cooperating with their neighbors. They accrete to form a structure a foot tall, only to separate once more into countless rugged little individualists."

Stryker activated an infrasonic signal generator – its output well below the threshold of the human ear – then threw a switch to engage a hidden motor. And as the metal door in the inlet slowly opened, the professor drew a large plastic bucket from a shelf, pried off the lid and tossed handfuls of pellets into the lab's central pool.

"My special blend," he said with a wry smile. "Guaranteed to produce healthier, happier lampreys in just seven days, or your money back. Our guests should be arriving any time now, and I have no doubt they'll be hungry."

The two men watched and waited as a rapidly moving mass of indeterminate size entered the inlet on the island's southwestern flank. An advancing pressure wave bulged the pool's surface as they drew near. "Ah, here they are now," said the professor.

An instant later an enormous column of lampreys erupted into the air amidst a geyser of water.

"Those look like the bastards that sank us!" Roland shouted, jumping aside and retreating into the antechamber filled with aquariums. Stryker stood his ground and watched, spellbound, as the living mass threw itself against the wall – tipping over and shattering every aquarium stacked against it on the other side – hurling water, flopping fish and broken glass across the floor.

The writhing swarm began to destroy everything in the lab – knocking over shelves laden with pharmaceuticals in glass jars, solar storage batteries and various pieces of equipment. Exhibiting the focused determination of an individual organism, the biomass attacked the holding tanks, gouging and gnawing until their walls collapsed. Thousands of gallons flooded out, a torrent of foaming chemicals that swept the young lamprey and swamp eels into the pool. Captives no longer, the twisting, spiraling creatures coursed through the channel and swam past the metal door, then navigated the length of the inlet and merged into the open waters of the lake.

Stryker felt giddy pride mixed with fear as the swarm wriggled closer. He tried to outflank them but a squirming cascade of lampreys blocked his path, forcing him a step closer to the pool. Now, filled with the desperate exaltation of a mad scientist confronted by his own creation run amok, Stryker recited the names of all the cinematic monsters he had known and loved as a child, "Frankenstein… Kong… Godzilla… Mothra… Gorgo… Rodan… Ghidora… the Beast from 20,000 Fathoms and now… Clamp!"

The newly christened undulated nearer, their fathomless black eyes fixed upon the human now standing at the lip of the pool. The lampreys opened their oral hoods in unison – a thousand moist crimson disks quivering with anticipation.

Roland watched the hideous drama from a safe distance, beyond the door.

"Get out now," said Stryker, "while there's still…"

But 'time' never had a chance.

The lampreys thrust forward and encircled Stryker's feet. More and more added their bodies to the heap, holding him tightly. Unable to extricate himself, Stryker stood transfixed as the ghastly, squirming mound grew larger, rising to his chest and pining his arms tightly beneath a living tourniquet. The lamprey atop the mound coiled its body around Stryker's neck and squeezed. Others applied their repulsive crimson disks to the man's contorted face. Dozens of teeth sank into both cheeks – crushing nose cartilage and puncturing the sinus cavities. Finally, the lampreys chewed open his cranium and thrust their blade-tipped tongues deep into his brain.

A cooperative mass no longer, the lampreys dropped away, one by one, each returning to the pool to begin the swim to the lake – deep-water protection for them and a gaping maw of oblivion for the man.

Chapter Thirty-Eight

Roland watched in silent horror as the lampreys dropped into the pool with their prize. Then he ran outside into the pitch black. Temporarily blinded by the lingering effects of the fluorescent lights, he picked his way across the broken glass and found the path, cursing with every bare-footed step. From there he descended through the woods, climbed over the fallen cedar's tangle of limbs and emerged from the forest.

Jade stepped from behind the altar-shaped rock and joined him on the dock.

"I'm so glad it's you," she said, giving him a hug. "I waited to be certain before I revealed myself. Where's Stryker?"

"He's dead. The swarm got him. It entered the channel and burst in through a pool in his lab. I watched them destroy everything, the same way they tore apart the cabin on the boat. Then they carried him off like an order of fish and chips. An awful sight, one I shan't soon forget. Don't know about you, but I've had enough of this bloody island!"

"You'll be pleased to hear we can take the rowboat to get away. I used an oar to pry away the board that held the chain."

"What a resourceful granddaughter you are."

"If we're careful, we might just slip away undetected."

Climbing aboard the little boat, Jade took the center seat and Roland the stern. She began to row as quietly as possible, navigating by starlight. Roland's night vision returned and was now as acute as Jade's as they maneuvered the length of the inlet, then out onto the open lake. He gazed at the glittering firmament overhead. Angled low in the south, the asterism formed by the constellation Sagittarius issued an eternal steam of vaporous starlight from the teapot's spout. A meteor streaked silently across the sky, leaving a glowing trail that faded a second later. Neither spoke as Jade rowed across the bay and towards the mainland, a trip that took about ten minutes.

"Terra firma at last," she said, as the bow scrunched onto the pebbled beach. "Care for a drink? I managed to save the last of the gin and tonic."

"Yes indeed, and I propose a toast to our late, misguided host," said Roland, taking a swig. "And to all who are consumed by the fruits of their labors, pun intended."

Roland and Jade sat in the peaceful darkness, passing the bottle back and forth and peering at the island – a dark hump slightly darker than the surrounding night.

A quarter mile away on the island, the propane continued to leak from the broken regulator. Gas flowed around the building's foundation and into the lab, where it mingled with volatile fumes escaping from dozens of broken solar-energy storage batteries. A spark from an imploded computer monitor ignited the mixture, unleashing one final Independence Day explosion, hurling rocks high into the air like a miniature reenactment of the destruction of Krakatau. A roiling ball of flame lit the night as debris splashed down in a wide radius.

The expanding shock wave awoke everyone within a 15-mile radius.

Fire ravaged the island, consuming every twig, branch and tree.

All traces of Stryker's citadel of science ceased to exist, except for bits of melted glass blown outward and scattered on the lake bottom. The shattered rocks surrounding a central crater would exhibit the effects of scorching till the next Ice Age.

Never again, neither day nor night, would Dark Island ever be quite as dark. The denuded outcrop would soon become known as Crater Island.

Chapter Thirty-Nine

Guests arriving at the Rock Cove resort on the morning of the fifth expressed incredulity upon hearing of the previous night's extraordinary events; but one look at the cove and the Ticonderoga's superstructure rising above the waterline quelled all doubts.

The stranded orchestra members had been ferried ashore during the night. Now, as the rising sun evaporated the dew-laden grass, Sergeant Edwards and Captain Griffis stood on the rock peninsula alongside the cove, watching as forensic specialists bagged the human remains being brought up by Police divers. Hundreds of dead lampreys littered the shallows nearby, their limp bodies rolling ever so slightly in the gentle swell.

"It's a miracle more people weren't killed," said the sergeant. "If they'd stayed onboard instead of trying to swim ashore, they'd still be alive."

"The Ticonderoga must've been taking on water continuously," replied the captain, "but so slowly no one noticed. Or maybe something in the hull gave way below the waterline. We won't know till she's raised and the engineers go over every inch with a fine-toothed comb. They should never have put her back in the water. I tried to warn them, but they wouldn't listen. If it was up to me, I'd leave her right where she is as a memorial."

The sergeant scratched the stubble on his chin and said, "They weren't the only one's who were warned."

The roving television news team was now onsite and Elsbeth was the first person to be interviewed. The resort's general manager gave every indication of being profoundly concerned, but still managed to deliver one masterful public relations sound bite after another, concluding with, "In spite of this tragic mishap, Rock Cove continues to offer an escape from the scurry and strife of the modern world. We invite you to come and enjoy Mother Nature's gentler side."

When the reporter moved on to question an eyewitness, the sergeant stepped into Elsbeth's path. "I hope you're satisfied," he said. "You ignored my entreaties and now at least ten more people are dead. I'm going to give the media a day to get a handle on all this, and then, I'll give them an exclusive interview that will expose you for the greedy insensitive bitch you are."

"Go ahead, you do that," she snapped. "Create as much fuss as possible. I'll spin it the other way and you'll be blamed for failing to uncover the cause of these attacks in time to prevent them. Either way, the resort will get a million dollars worth of free advertising. The phone's already ringing off the hook with reservations, so there's no need to worry about the resort's fiscal survival."

"The families of the victims will be thrilled to hear it. But mark my words, next time you may not be so impervious."

"How could there possibly be a next time?"

"Count on it, Elsbeth. There's always a next time."

* * *

News of Stryker's death spread quickly among the many marine biologists that gathered at the cove to collect lamprey carcasses for dissection and analysis. Speculation as to why the murderous swarm formed, or why it succumbed in an orgy of sudden death dominated their conversation. None had yet to forge a link between Stryker and the unprecedented attacks, but all agreed that serious effort would have to be made to determine why the lampreys had become resistant to the lampricide used against them as larva.

While some suspected tolerance to Zentiloft as a result of mutation, and others questioned the chemical's potency, no one had yet to experience the blinding flash of the obvious – the realization that just before the mass die-off, the swarm had spawned, releasing countless sperm and egg cells into the water, just as salmon have always done after migrating to the waters of their origin.

Soon, the debate among the scientists would rage over whether or not the next generation would possess the same nasty characteristics displayed by their late forbearers. All agreed, however, that fertilized eggs would have to be acquired and allowed to mature; for without living specimens to study, there was little to do except theorize.

According to the police report, an explosion (known by firefighters as a BLEVE, a Boiling Liquid Evaporation Event) killed Stryker and eliminated all traces of his remains.

Most of the instruments owned by the members of the Green Mountain Philharmonic had been carried to safety when the musicians crowded onto the Ticonderoga's upper deck. The larger and heavier ones, alas, remained on the lower deck and were damaged by the water.

After a thorough cleaning and new pads, the brass instruments would sing again. Sadly, the harp sustained harm serious enough to require a year to repair, and even then the instrument would never fully regain its self-assurance.

The cellos, violas and violins survived, but the string basses suffered the greatest depredations: Some floated away like doghouses in the great flood of 1927. All required extensive repairs after the hide glue let go and the instruments collapsed.

For the rest of the summer, people would occasionally find odd souvenirs floating here and there around the lake – bow ties or sheets of music drifting like fallen leaves. Skin divers would occasionally come up with one of the black shoes that lay on the cove's bottom like so many patent-leather clams. And for years to come, amateur scuba divers would search in vain for the fabled "lost Steinway," rumored to have gone down with the ship.

The Green Mountain Philharmonic enjoyed a tremendous increase in ticket sales as a result of the disaster and the ensuing publicity. Even so, the orchestra's board of directors placed a permanent moratorium on all floating concerts.

Maestro von Hesse retired to his farm in the Northeast Kingdom to raise sheep.

Squirrels in the Attic never recovered from the loss of Charlie, although the surviving members went on to join other bands.

The Globster's bones were found and his name added to the list of casualties.

The Moira would be patched, pumped out and towed to a shipyard for repairs, although the insurance agent would squawk long and loud before finally attributing the damage to vandalism.

The disappearance of Larry Providence would remain a mystery until one of the police divers heard about the abandoned cart found near the water hazard on the resort's ninth hole. The officer postulated that the pond had become infested with lampreys as a result of the shallow trench that connected it to the lake.

Neither they, nor the lampreys in Harvey's pool were exempt from the compulsion to reproduce and perish. The new generation conceived in the pond had a chance of survival, however, but those trapped in the pool were doomed.

Chapter Forty

Things were buzzing at the Krampton Kountry store when Sergeant Edwards stopped in to buy a quart of milk and a dozen powdered doughnuts – a rare indulgence – before returning to police headquarters. Clearly exhausted, he listened as Howard and Marion discussed the previous night's apocalyptic events and the musician's fatal swim – without question the greatest mother lode for gossip in the town's long history.

Abe was there too, listening with growing annoyance to their account, wishing he hadn't left early to avoid a soaking. "That's what spooked my herd the day they kicked the wall down," he concluded, after hearing about the 'Ti going down and the lamprey attack. "They must've swum up from the lake and gotten into the cow's drinking water!"

"The lampreys were responsible for Thad's death," said Marion. "And the disappearance of Hank and Zeke and the Spaulding twins and everything else that's gone wrong around here."

Howard turned up the volume on the television. Everyone in the store turned to watch the live update being broadcast from the resort: The earnest young reporter onscreen furrowed her brow and did her best to look insightful, then took a breath and began . . .

"In addition to the bizarre events here at the Rock Cove Resort that resulted in the deaths of nine members of the Green Mountain Philharmonic and the leader of the band, Squirrels in the Attic, a massive explosion claimed the life of Dr. Stanley Stryker, marine biologist, UVM professor and longtime Krampton resident. We do not yet know the cause of the blast that destroyed his home and swept Dark Island of all life. On a brighter note, we've received numerous reports of Champ sightings in recent days. We have no new pictures at this time but we're keeping our fingers crossed."

Howard switched off the set.

Just then the screen door opened and in walked Snee. The fellow looked as thin and grizzled as ever but seemed somehow different, as if a subtle transformation had taken place, a change immediately apparent to Howard and Marion.

Snee gazed at them as if at long lost friends suddenly reunited. "I awoke this morning in a strange bed in a strange cottage," he said. "At first I didn't know where I was, or who I was. Then I remembered... I'm Thomas

M. Snee, artist and art historian. It's incredible, but I seem to have recovered my wits."

* * *

Later that afternoon Roland telephoned Waves and said, "I intend to continue the search for Champ, once I've returned from a brief but necessary trip to London. I mustn't allow my funding for our little quest to terminate, especially now. Before leaving, however, I have one request and a rather important one at that. I want you to stay off the lake. Don't go boating or swimming. I know this sounds daft but I can't explain now; I have a plane to catch and I'm running late. Jade will fill you in on the details, but promise me you'll do as I ask."

"All right," said Waves, "but if anyone else had made such an oddball request, I'd laugh in their face and hang up. Coming from you, though... I consent."

"Good show. Now I must push off. I'll call as soon as I'm back."

After driving to the resort, Waves stood on the deck attached to the cottage named Tranquility and listened to Jade's account of the previous night's singular events.

"Wait," he interrupted, "before you say another word, where's my boat?"

"I was just getting to that," she said. "We ran into a spot of bother, as Roland would say. I was underwater, conducting an inspection of Stryker's island when I was attacked by a swarm of lampreys. I fought back and suddenly they broke off and swam away. But then, after I was back onboard, they chewed through the hull and sank us."

"You sank my boat?"

"Yes. I'm afraid she might be totaled."

"Totaled! What happened, did you hit a buoy, or was Champ having a bad day?"

"No! I'm telling you the truth, hundreds of lampreys gnawed through the hull. The Moira settled at an angle in shallow water and we clung to the bowsprit. I'm really sorry, but it wasn't my fault. We were trapped and there was nothing we could do."

"How did you escape?"

"After the storm, Stryker picked us up in a rowboat and brought us, at gunpoint, to the island. But I managed to slip away."

"Where is Stryker now?"

"The swarm ate him. We were lucky; we rowed across to the mainland just minutes before the explosion destroyed everything on the island."

"Last night turned into a nightmare here as well. The orchestra onboard the Ticonderoga played while it sank, just like the Titanic; then the lampreys killed some of the musicians when they tried to swim ashore. They got Charlie, our singer, too."

Waves pulled Jade into his arms and held her tightly. She returned the hug, which evolved into an embrace, and then a lengthy kiss.

"I'm glad you weren't eaten," he said, after they came up for air.

Chapter Forty-One

A perfect summer day seemed to not only promise but deliver eternal youth as Waves and Jade launched a canoe onto the tranquil waters of Dead Creek. Serenaded by the songs of unseen birds, they paddled upstream against a current so gentle as to appear nonexistent, gliding between lush, tree-lined banks separated by 40 feet of water still turgid after the most recent rain.

Darning needles unchanged for millions of years hovered and zoomed. From time to time the sun broke through the forest canopy, illuminating the vestiges of morning mist. The canoe glided past hayfields basking in the sun, their margins giving way to wetlands ruled by beavers.

"Roland told us to stay off the lake," said Waves, "but he never said a word about the river."

"That's true," Jade replied. "Although the lake has been quiet since the Fourth. Look, there's a heron, standing on one leg. This is much better than looking at scenery through a car window, even if it is a Jaguar. How far upstream will we go?"

"There's a magnificent waterfall a couple of miles ahead, a great place for a picnic. It'll take us an hour to get there. And with any luck we'll have it all to ourselves."

"What will your band do without a singer? Will you try to find a replacement?"

"No, Charlie was one of a kind. I'll have to start looking for another band."

They paddled in silence, their thoughts suddenly diverted by the fragility of life.

* * *

Although Stryker was gone forever, his progeny lived on. The lampreys and swamp eels liberated from the lab on that cataclysmic night had dispersed widely, but, being unaccustomed to having to hunt for food, they now experienced the persistent, aching emptiness of hunger.

A new swarm of lampreys began to accrete below the surface – mutants all, but mutations rarely create improvements; most result in a defect that selects the bearer for extinction, preventing the propagation of that weakness to the next generation. But for the lampreys now gathering, the mutation accelerated their growth and maturation.

Shunning the sunlit waters near the surface, they lurked in the depths and preyed upon the few remaining fish – the trout, bass and pike that had hitherto occupied the second tier on the food chain. Their strength increased with every feeding, but the depleted fish population declined still further, forcing the lampreys and swamp eels to turn upon one another. Driven by insatiable appetite, a roiling mass of sinuous bodies fought in deep water. These deadly skirmishes ceased only when it became time for the survivors to heed the genetic command to slake a more profound hunger – the urge to reproduce.

* * *

Waves and Jade completed their canoe trip upstream; the roaring sound of the waterfalls reached their ears before it met their eyes – a flume cascading into a deep pool flanked by moss-covered cliffs shining with moisture.

"Here we are," said Waves.

"A magical place," said Jade. "I'll bet the fireflies dance here at night."

"Yes, and the mosquitoes too."

After beaching the canoe on a spit of sand, they gathered up their supplies and climbed the flat rocks that ascended like stairs, a veritable midget's causeway leading to a promontory overlooking the wide pool. Each step they took provoked a dash by exceedingly agile wolf spiders seeking new and presumably better places to hide. The sun would soon clear the trees and bathe the rocks with sufficient energy to keep them warm till long after sunset.

Waves spread the blanket as Jade emptied the wicker basket – a Bohemian banquet comprised of smoked oysters, a wedge of cheddar cheese, a loaf of French bread, carrots, olives, celery with peanut butter smeared the length of each grooved stalk, grapes, corn chips and a bottle of a decent Merlot. For desert, imported dark chocolate and two crisp apples. Waves uncorked the wine.

"May I ply you with alcohol?"

"Please do," said Jade, her aviator style sunglasses glinting in the sunlight.

Waves filled two plastic cups, handed one to her and said, "To the good ship Moira, which, incidentally, has been in the shipyard for a week, being overhauled."

"And to the insurance company that's going to pay for it," Jade replied.

They sipped the wine and congratulated one another on having the good sense to visit such a beautiful spot. Then they began to eat, crunching celery and nibbling carrots like lusty young rabbits. Waves stabbed one smoked oyster after another with a plastic fork and wondered if their rumored effects as an aphrodisiac were true. As if reading his mind, Jade removed her shirt and stripped off her shorts to reveal tanned flesh confined by only the most diminutive purple bikini. Her skin looked as smooth and taut as the outer wrapping on a dolphin.

"What month were you born?" Waves asked.

"Can't you tell? I'm a Piscean. What about you? What's your sign?"

"O positive."

"Seriously, what sign?"

"I'll tell you when we're better acquainted."

"Is that so? All kidding aside, I'd like to know what you most want out of life."

Waves took a sip of the Merlot and considered the question.

"Let's see, now," he began. "Once I've attained fame, wealth and the respect of my peers, I want a woman, not any woman, mind you, but one with a bold sense of style; someone who has not been smothered by good taste – a woman who adorns her body with a cloak of golden sequins, not an old brown saddle blanket thrown over the hide of a llama. Know what I mean?"

"Absolutely."

He swallowed more wine and warmed to the subject.

"I want a woman with whom I can dance the mambo till dawn and then stagger home through the streets, singing our heads off. And most of all, I want to weave a mat of pubic hair so I can get down on my knees and worship sex!"

Jade laughed and said, "Wrong! What you want most out of life is sex."

Waves blushed and said, "I suppose you're right, but I was trying to be a gentleman."

"Keep trying," she replied. "But it's good to meet a man who knows what he wants."

"You bet. Now it's your turn. What do you want from life? And what do you do when you're not designing software or hacking killer lampreys to pieces?"

Jade spat an olive pit over the ledge before answering. "First, I want more wine and a swim. Then I'll tell you."

"Fair enough," said Waves, refilling her glass. "There are two ways to enter the water; gradually – down by the canoe – or you can hurl yourself over the edge like a lemming. The water's quite deep and there's no dangerous undertow to worry about. Personally, I prefer the lemming technique. Stripping off his shirt and sneakers, he took several steps back, then sprinted across the plateau and leapt into gravity's embrace. Not about to be outdone, Jade stood on the edge of the precipice for a moment, then performed a perfect swan dive, knifing cleanly into the water with toes pointed and hardly a splash.

"A nine point five," said Waves.

The couple cavorted in the refreshingly cool water until Waves swam to the rocky perimeter, climbed out and opened the knapsack he'd left in the canoe. "Here," he said, handing Jade a mask and a pair of fins. "I want to show you something."

Donning the gear, they swam underwater and marveled at the sight of falling water striking the surface; seen from below – a blue-tinged cauldron of bubbles radiating from a restless epicenter. After surfacing Waves shouted, "Follow me," above the roaring downdraft. He swam across the pool and emerged alongside the cataract. "We'll leave the mask and flips here," he said, before climbing the wet rocks to a ledge and stepping behind the curtain of water into a cave.

A deep throb like a low E from an organ pipe trembled in the air as they explored the cave's moist, dim recesses. At the innermost point the junction of walls, floor and ceiling created a cozy niche where a saber-toothed tiger might conceivably curl up for a nap.

* * *

The swarm entered the mouth of Dead Creek. Driven by genetic determinism implanted as zygotes, they surged upstream, propelled by powerful thrusts of their tails. They followed the river's many twists and soon reached the deep pool beneath the falls. There, a thousand lampreys circulated through the water, their bioelectric senses revealing little more than each other's bodies.

* * *

"This is fantastic," said Jade. "We could live in here! It's perfect. I could invent fire and raise our grubby brood while you hunt and gather. In our spare time we could chisel images of Jaguar convertibles into the cave walls."

"Sounds good to me. Someday anthropologists will discover our bones and your sunglasses. Although I'm not too sure about the bikini."

Troglodytes no longer, they reemerged into broad daylight and stood on the ledge, watching the water's hypnotic plunge. Climbing down the slippery rocks was more difficult than ascending, but they took their time, then retrieved their skin-diving gear and jumped once more into the deep pool.

The swarm circulated rapidly beneath them. Their slippery, cold flanks brushed against Jade's legs and an adrenalin-spiked shot of fear coursed through her veins when she realized they were not alone. She waved her arms and shouted to signal, but Waves floated on his back, unable to see or hear her entreaties.

She swam over to him, punched his arm and yelled, "The lampreys are here!"

He lowered the mask over his face, dipped beneath the surface and saw the dense moving mass as it slewed by, driving the water into a massive rotating whirlpool.

"Swim to the rocks!" shouted Jade.

They fought against the tumultuous, rotating current but were caught in the maelstrom's grip. Every time they attempted to force their way through, the swarm pushed them back, knocking their masks off, but not the fins, which enabled them to keep their heads above the surface.

Oblivious to all but their own purpose, the lampreys surrendered to the ancient rhythms of procreation. Thousands of sinuously twisting bodies swam as one, driven by the irresistible pressure to drain seminal vesicles and ovaries swollen with eggs. Theirs was not a quick, utilitarian ejaculation, but a frenzy that gradually built to an imminent threshold. Once achieved, hormones squirted to trigger powerful contractions. Out poured millions of microscopic eggs and sperm – gallons of living genetic material that clouded the water with a milky curtain.

Waves and Jade fought to remain afloat as the lampreys writhed and twisted and foamed the water, insuring the blending of the two substances, the first step in the creation of myriad zygotes.

And then it was over.

The lampreys separated and swam downstream; each intent upon reaching the mouth of the creek and dispersing once more into the lake's black depths. The whirlpool slowed and disappeared.

Waves and Jade floated amidst the milky pool, alone once more.

"They're gone," he said. "Ugh! Is this stuff what I think it is?"

"Yes indeed," answered Jade with a crazed grin on her face. "Genuine, one hundred percent, high-octane lamprey jism!"

"Jade, you'll always be a barracuda among Pisceans."

They swam to the rocks at the water's edge and rinsed the sticky residue from their limbs and hair. Only then did they realize that the canoe was gone.

"The current created by the swarm must've dislodged it," Waves surmised.

"Should we forge through the woods on foot or swim downstream and try to find it?"

"I thought you wanted to live in the cave," said Waves. "Here's your chance."

"I may have to revise that wish."

"So, the first hint of trouble and it's back to the comforts of civilization?"

"That was more than a hint."

Waves and Jade climbed out of the pool, ascended the rock steps and sat on the warm blanket.

"Look here," said Waves, "we still have plenty of bread and water."

"How appropriate, but I'm not hungry – at least not for food. Isn't it time we spawned?"

But before any blood could be diverted from its usual circulatory route to the appropriate organs, they heard the familiar thrum of an inboard V8 engine. They turned to watch as the Moira slowed to a halt in the pool beneath the falls. Roland waved, pointed to the long green object tied across the transom and said, "I say, have either of you lost a canoe?"

Chapter Forty-Two

After acknowledging the astonishing return of his wits, and thanking them for their kindness, Snee bid good day to Howard and Marion, thereby giving the gossipmongers yet another revelation to disseminate in this bumper crop year for the grapevine. Sergeant Edwards departed soon thereafter, earnestly hoping that he'd seen the last of Krampton. The officer climbed into his cruiser and drove away, passing Snee as he walked along, for once without his bicycle.

Ten minutes later, Snee approached the barbed wire fence that formed the eastern boundary to Abe's farmland. The herd stood grazing a long way off and there were no dangerous bulls to contend with, so, rather than hike the long way around to his campsite, Snee decided to cut across the pasture. A fallen tree limb depressed the fence's top strand, providing a convenient low spot where he could swing one leg over and then the other. Ever curious, the cows turned their heads to watch.

Snee munched an apple as he walked, keeping one eye open for fresh cow pies and the other eye on the herd. The cows began to amble towards him, their hooves indenting the moist earth with every step. When they quickened their pace, Snee increased his. When the herd started trotting, he followed suit; and when the cows broke into a run, the painter bolted like a rabbit.

The Holsteins were intrigued; never before had they witnessed a human abdicate all pretense of authority by fleeing at their approach. A grove of maple trees beckoned from a football field's length away as Snee ran on spindly shanks unused to such pursuit. The cows quickly closed the distance, prancing and mooing at the realization that chasing people is fun!

Snee slipped on a disk of partially dried manure and stumbled headlong on what would've been the 30-yard line. He lay there for a moment while the herd bore down upon him, and then, after envisioning the headlines in the Bulwagga Beacon, "ARTIST TRAMPLED TO DEATH BY COWS," he got to his feet, turned and faced his pursuers. The herd slowed its advance as he pulled another apple from his jacket pocket, took aim and hurled the shiny Macintosh at the obstreperous beast leading the charge. The apple flew through the air and struck the cow's speckled nose with a surprisingly loud bonk!

Bull's eye, he thought, or rather, cow's eye.

But instead of being intimidated, the cow bellowed with indignation. The entire herd joined in, then charged like angry rhinos taunted by an impudent hyena. Snee took to his heels once more and dashed for the trees. He grabbed the lowest branch and hauled himself up just seconds before the herd thundered to a halt beneath him. They gathered round the trunk, raised their shaggy heads and glared.

The treed trespasser pondered his predicament, then looked around and spotted Abe's farmhouse hundreds of yards away, well beyond shouting range. Snee realized that he had no choice but to sit there like a baboon, eat his last apple and wait for the herd to grow bored and wander off. The cows had nothing else to do and all the time in the world to do it, so they decided to sit beneath the maple trees and enjoy the shade.

* * *

The Asian swamp eels prowled through lake water devoid of fish. Hunger goaded them on as they swam to the nearest shore from varying radii. They followed the water's edge until the cliffs gave way to the gently sloping margins of the land. There, the eels left the water and insinuated their way, one at a time, into the adjacent fields of hay, alfalfa and corn. Their moist skin quickly toughened into a protective membrane. Surprisingly acute vision now became their primary sense, eyes alert for any movement that might signal the presence of small, edible creatures.

The eels moved at a pace considerably slower and less graceful than in water; some moved across a green carpet of vegetation, others on bare dirt, their progress slow but steady.

A foraging raccoon encountered an eel. Unsure as to its capacity for defense, the coon warily observed its quarry before attacking. A furious tussle ensued as the eel coiled its muscular body around the animal like a miniature anaconda. The eel excreted a noxious layer of mucus, thwarting any chance of receiving a fatal bite. Unnerved, the raccoon struggled free and loped away, its fur matted with a sticky paste that irritated its eyes and muzzle.

The eel moved on and passed beneath the lowest strand of a barbed wire fence. Ahead lay hundreds of acres of corn – endless rows of rustling stalks dense enough to shield it from the sharp eyes of airborne predators, and tall enough to hide a man running for his life. The eel turned perpendicularly to the tasseled green ranks and pushed forward with repetitive side-to-side thrusts that eventually brought it into Abe's pasture.

Thirty-eight cows drowsed peacefully in the shade, but grew increasingly skittish when they noticed the squirming, yard-long intruder in their midst. The herd rose to its feet and galloped into the far corner of the pasture, provoked, no doubt, by the memory of lampreys in the barn's water trough, snapping at their vulnerable pink noses.

* * *

Inside Abe's house, the exhausted dairyman lay stretched out on the parlor couch, napping intermittently while the Nature Channel ran a documentary on reptiles. It had been a long day, and with the second milking yet to be done, it was only half over. Abe had been unable to find reliable help after the disappearance of Hank and Zeke, forcing him to do all the work himself. As a result, he suffered the aches and twinges brought on by ceaseless toil and increasing decrepitude.

Abe woke to the sound of Rocky's wheezing woof. He eased himself off the couch, switched off the television and pulled the screen door open to let the dog out. Although it was still only mid-afternoon, he turned and trudged up the stairs to his bedroom, vowing once more to move his bed to the empty room on the first floor. Once in his bedroom, the old farmer kicked off his slippers, collapsed onto the bed and drifted off.

* * *

Still perched in the tree, Snee watched as the herd galloped away, trampling and squashing the eel to death. He was about to climb down when he observed more eels approaching and passing beneath, a migration unlike any he'd ever seen, all moving in the direction of Abe's house.

Snee did not like their looks at all. Each eel was thick and muscular, and there was something sinister in the way they moved – not the smooth, effortless glide of a snake, but an awkward, lurching, forward thrust. He decided to sit there a while longer and wait till the eels had gone.

The branch had become a very uncomfortable seat by the time Snee decided to continue his walk across the pasture. He eased himself to the ground like some anthropological missing link, pausing to peer at the dead eel for a moment, and then set off at a brisk pace. Curiosity got the better of him and he changed course and headed towards Abe's house.

* * *

Rocky stepped off the porch and sniffed the air about the time the first eel entered the yard. Although the dog's eyesight was failing, his sense of smell remained acute and he detected the eel's peculiar scent, beyond the acuity of human noses but blatant to a canine. Rocky pounced and seized the eel in his jaws, killing it with several vigorous shakes. Much too large to swallow, the collie dropped the limp carcass and settled down to defend the yard from further invasion.

Rocky didn't have long to wait. More eels arrived – individually, but regularly – and every time one crossed onto the lawn, Rocky was there to meet it.

The old dog hadn't had so much fun or exertion in ages – biting eel after eel – thrashing and killing each one before it could excrete protective mucus. Rocky dispatched more than a dozen before growing tired and withdrawing to the porch. The assault seemed to have ended, so he pushed the screen door open with his head and entered the quiet house, then climbed the stairs and flopped onto the rug at the foot of Abe's bed, his preferred place for sleeping.

* * *

Another wave of eels crossed onto the lawn. Solitary arrivals no longer, they arrived in two's and three's – an onslaught that paused to consume their fallen brethren, before continuing on towards the house. The eels ascended the porch steps and pressed against the screen door, pushing it open wide enough to squeeze through. The growing horde wriggled across the parlor floor, an expanse of scuffed, brown linoleum considered stylish when it was laid down in 1952.

The eels ranged throughout the ground floor, drawn by the residual odor of man, dog and cat, then into the kitchen. The wood trim around the doorway was worn smooth and shiny, much the way the interior of a bear's den is burnished by years of contact with a greasy ursine hide. A pantry opened on one side, its shelves stocked with jars of beans, beets and pickles – nothing remotely appealing to hungry, carnivorous eels. The banister and the stairs leading up to the second floor were especially redolent of humanity. The stairs, however, presented an insuperable barrier to creatures that relied upon a lurching, side-to-side method of propulsion. Instead, they snapped peevishly at one another.

The hinged pet door into the kitchen opened and closed as Abe's favorite cat stepped through. The charcoal gray tabby walked across the floor to the bowl with the name "Esther" on its side. Suddenly an eel lunged out of a dim corner. The cat sprang three feet into the air, landed with all claws extended and zipped away. But instead of escaping through the pet door, Esther raced into the parlor, leapt from the couch to an overstuffed chair and rocketed around the room without once touching the floor. Several eels lashed out but missed as the cat launched herself into the air and landed on the mantle-piece, bumping into and sending an antique Staffordshire dog crashing to the floor.

Rocky and Abe both awoke at the sound of porcelain shattering, and the dog began to bark. Abe's first suspicion centered on a clumsy burglar at work, but when the second porcelain dog smashed to the floor, he wasn't so sure. The elderly farmer opened his closet door and grabbed a shotgun – a double-barrel, small-bore, fowling piece designed to bring down pheasant. Abe opened a box of shells, loaded the gun and stuffed a handful of extra shells in his pocket while Rocky stood on the landing and barked his head off.

"I'm coming down and I've got a shotgun!" Abe hollered, hoping the warning would drive the intruder away. "I'm gonna' shoot first and ask questions later!"

The eels moved towards the foot of the stairs as Abe descended. Halfway down he saw sudden, unidentifiable movement and discharged both barrels, splattering eel fragments against the wall and evoking another loud screech from Esther as she stood atop the mantle – her back arched, teeth bared and fur erect. Abe reloaded and fired once more into the wriggling mass, then reloaded and descended another step.

* * *

Snee heard the shotgun blasts but was unsure whether or not to risk a closer look. Curiosity overcame reticence. He approached the farmyard just as Abe reached the bottom of the steps. The frenzy in the parlor intensified as the numerous remaining eels twisted and lunged. Abe unleashed another deafening fusillade of steel pellets that tore through their flesh and scattered bloody pieces all over the room.

"There's a bite in the old dog yet!" Abe shouted, inserting more shells, snapping the breach closed and firing again and again. Rocky grabbed an eel, shook it violently and then bit it in half, thereby confirming his master's boast. Esther hissed and spat as each blast ripped more eels apart, spraying slimy bits all over the curtains, windows and walls.

Another salvo killed the last of the eels inside the house.

* * *

Snee ducked behind a fake wishing well in Abe's yard and listened to the shotgun blasts. Unwilling to expose himself to such pandemonium, he crouched there long enough to give a number of late-arriving eels an easy target. Their clumsy advance caught Snee's eye and he backed away. But now, standing in the open, he became the focal point for every eel within a range of a hundred feet.

The gathering eels moved closer, forcing him to retreat towards the cornfield.

The barbed wire fence there was too tall to step over so he forced the middle two strands apart with his hands, put one leg through, and then his head and shoulders. Snee raised his other leg and brought it through, but a sharp, pointed barb hooked his jacket and held him fast. He fought against the restraint, aware of the eels drawing near.

He kicked away the first and second eels to reach the fence, then struggled free of his jacket and dashed headlong into the cornfield like a scarecrow come to life, leaving the tattered garment behind, hanging on the wire.

Epilogue

The lampreys left behind the turgid waters of Dead Creek and scattered, descending into the somber depths before settling on the barren lakebed. Having expended the last of their energy, undulant coiling ceased and they lay still. Their bioelectric senses lapsed into torpor. Respiration grew increasingly sluggish and ceased. Death claimed the lampreys, but their fertilized eggs were already undergoing mitosis, dividing again and again in the sheltered waters of Dead Creek. It would be years before this new generation would abandon the river, but the intervening time would allow the lake's depleted fish population to recover.

In the meantime, life continued to flourish, as it has for countless millennia. With the exception of plants and the pallid tubeworms clustered around scalding geothermal vents on the ocean floor, survival for both macro and micro remained dependent upon two basic principles, rules as simple as they were antediluvian: Kill or be killed, eat or be eaten.

The only compensation for this unremitting carnage, however ephemeral, was the distraction provided by the equally unrelenting reproductive imperative – a sacred ritual performed by every creature that twitches, slithers, lopes or flies.

The challenge was to survive. The only reward for doing so was the opportunity to spume forth the pulse of the next generation, be it tail-lashing spermatozoa bearing genetic telegrams, or the release of spores, cysts, embryos, larva and fully formed young. And once jettisoned, they, too pirouetted in the center ring of the great circus of Existence. For the duration of little more than one blink of the cosmic eye, they gorged upon nectar before joining the silent multitudes already embarked upon that long, slow trudge across the dreary, horizonless plain of extinction.

The depths of Lake Champlain remain inhospitable to all who breathe without the benefit of gills. The deep water is perpetually cold and dark – a null zone untouched by the faintest insinuation of light, a black totality made all the more forbidding during the long hours of night. For there, in the deepest stygian vaults, senses other than sight have been relied upon for vast epochs far exceeding man's puny cognitive grasp.

For now, Lake Champlain is tranquil. The ferries run on-schedule. Small boats dot the surface and swimmers encounter nothing more threatening than zebra mussels. Fishermen catch bony perch, while golden retrievers dash into the water after sticks with impunity.

The surface continues to exhibit its normal complement of moods, seething with wind-swept turbulence one day, calm the next, sometimes as bright and reflective as an alien sea filled with boiling mercury. At other times, as frozen and quiescent as the surface of the Jovian moon Europa.

But on this particular evening the rising full moon scattered sequins upon the water's surface while hungry swamp eels moved inland. And as the moon gained altitude it turned from a pale, yellow disk to a bright ivory orb that illuminated the mist rising from the ground.

Darkened houses stood between the fields and along dirt lanes not far from the lake. Many sheltered families – husbands, wives and children tucked in their beds, snug and secure in the knowledge that nothing can harm them.

The eels rippled through the dew-moistened grass, moving ever closer.

Printed in the United States
105716LV00009B/55-75/A

9 781601 452818